"You do your job, I'll do mine."

"Maybe that isn't what I want." His eyes skimmed her body, lingering on the curve of her breast under the clinging top. His gaze seemed to touch her like a caressing hand, reminding her with nerve-shattering potency how, only a few hours before, she'd lain half-naked and wholly vulnerable in his arms.

"You're going to have to accept my presence— whether you like it or not."

She moved restlessly. "For how long?"

His meditative glance swept her, sending another quiver of uneasiness through her body. "As long as it takes."

SARA CRAVEN probably had the ideal upbringing for a budding writer. She grew up by the seaside in a house crammed with books, a box of old clothes to dress up in and a swing outside in a walled garden. She produced the opening of her first book at age five and is eternally grateful to her mother for having kept a straight face! Sara now lives in France with her husband and two basset hounds.

Books by Sara Craven

HARLEQUIN PRESENTS
1176—KING OF SWORDS
1241—ISLAND OF THE HEART
1279—FLAWLESS
1330—STORM FORCE
1471—WHEN THE DEVIL DRIVES
1503—DESPERATE MEASURES
1549—DARK RANSOM

Sara Craven

DAWN SONG

Harlequin Books

TORONTO • NEW YORK • LONDON
AMSTERDAM • PARIS • SYDNEY • HAMBURG
STOCKHOLM • ATHENS • TOKYO • MILAN
MADRID • WARSAW • BUDAPEST • AUCKLAND

ISBN 0-373-11640-3

DAWN SONG

CHAPTER ONE

'IT'S the perfect solution. You can go in my place.'

Margot Trant's airy remark was followed by a silence that could have been cut by a knife.

Meg Langtry cleared her throat. 'Let me get this straight,' she said slowly. 'You want me to go to the south of France next month and stay at your godmother's château, pretending to be you.' She paused, giving her stepsister a long, steady look. 'Those are the basic elements of the scenario?'

'Well, what's wrong with that?' Margot demanded. 'The old bag wants someone to keep her company for four weeks while her regular slave has a well-deserved break. As long as someone turns up claiming to be Margot Trant, what problem can there possibly be?'

'Oh, none of course,' Meg returned with terrible irony. 'The fact that we don't even look alike is quite immaterial.'

Margot shrugged. 'I'm blonde—you're brunette.' She gave Meg's simply styled fall of brown hair a disparaging look. 'That can be easily fixed.

As for the rest—Tante's practically blind—that's why she needs a companion. You'll just be a blur.'

'Always my ultimate ambition,' Meg murmured.

Margot leaned forward. 'Oh, come on, Meg.' Her voice sharpened. 'You could do it easily. You'll have no job to worry about once that grotty second-hand bookshop you work for closes at the end of the week. And I can't possibly get away. You must see that.'

'Why not?' Meg countered. 'I thought Parliament "rose" in the summer. Surely Steven would give you leave.'

'Probably, if I asked him.' Margot's pretty face was suddenly intense. 'But he's just on the point of asking Corinne for a divorce. I simply can't afford to be away at this juncture.'

'I see,' Meg murmured drily. However distasteful she might personally find it, this was what her stepsister had been working towards, ever since she'd got the job as secretary to Steven Curtess MP, the young back-bencher who was being tipped for junior ministerial rank in the next government.

'And Godmother has no right to summon me like this—right out of the blue,' Margot went on petulantly. 'Good God, I haven't seen her since I was nine.'

'I wondered why I'd never heard of her.'

Margot hunched a shoulder. 'She's my great-aunt, actually—Dad was her favourite nephew, and I was named for her. So we're all three of us called Margaret,' she added triumphantly. 'Isn't that convenient?'

'Amazing.' Meg shook her head. 'But irrelevant. Wouldn't it be simpler just to write and tell her that you can't get away?'

'No, it would be extremely stupid,' Margot snapped. 'She has no children, and no other living relative as far as I know. And a château in the Languedoc isn't to be sneezed at as an inheritance. It's imperative I keep on the right side of her.' She gave Meg a suddenly limpid smile. 'Or that you do, on my behalf.'

'No way.' Meg bit her lip. 'Ethical considerations aside, we'd never get away with it.'

'Of course we would. Margot Trant is sent for. Margot Trant, presumably, turns up on the appointed day. And you're far better suited to running round after some dreary old lady than I'd ever be. Keep her sweet for me, and I'll be eternally grateful.'

'That's just the incentive I need, of course,' Meg said levelly. She pushed back her chair. 'You're the total limit, Margot. Do your own dirty work.'

'Oh, are you going?' Margot inspected a fleck on her fingernail. 'I thought the bookshop closed on Wednesdays.'

'It does. I'm spending the day with Nanny Turner, as I usually do.'

'Of course, in that sweet little cottage of hers—or should I say ours?'

There was a pause. Meg's eyes narrowed. 'Brydons Cottage is Nanny's for life,' she said. 'My father made that clear before he died.'

'Yes, but not in writing, sweetie. There's nothing legally binding. Oddly enough, Mummy was looking into it all the other day. Some friends of hers, the Nestors, are looking for a weekend place, and Brydons would be ideal.'

Meg stared at her. 'You're not serious? Nanny adores that cottage.'

'I bet she does,' Margot said acidly. 'It's a very desirable property.'

'But she'd have nowhere else to go.'

Margot's face was a mask of malice. 'There's always Sandstead House. Mummy has friends on the Social Services Committee. I'm sure they could pull a few strings.'

Meg drew a shaken breath. 'It would kill her to be in a home. She's terrific—firing on all cylinders. She can look after herself.'

'Then the choice is yours.' Margot spoke with cool finality. 'Go to the Languedoc in my place, and I'll persuade Mummy that it would be a betrayal of your father's memory to turn Nanny out.'

'That would make a difference?' Meg asked wrily.

'Oh, yes, she was awfully fond of him, even if she didn't go a bundle on Nanny and her bossy ways,' Margot said with insouciance. 'Besides, I'm the blue-eyed girl at the moment, and I know I can talk her round if I want. Mummy's dying to have a son-in-law in the government.'

And to hell with Corinne Curtess and the children, presumably, Meg thought grimly.

'I'll even get her to put something in writing about Nanny's tenure if you get through the month with Godmother none the wiser,' Margot wheedled. 'I need your help, Meg. I've got to stay here and keep the pressure on Steven.'

'If I do this,' Meg said icily, 'it will be for Nanny's sake—not to further your affair with a married man.'

'Oh, don't be so bloody pompous.' Margot stretched luxuriously. 'You'll be getting a whole month abroad in France, all expenses paid, at the height of the season. What more could you want?' She sent Meg a complacent smile. 'I'll even lend you my car to drive over to Nanny's. You'll need to practise your driving for France.'

Meg set her teeth. 'I haven't said I'm going yet.'

Margot's smile became almost cat-like. 'But you will,' she said. 'Or poor old Nanny becomes homeless. It's up to you.'

A fortnight later, Meg, much against her better judgement, was on her way.

She'd intended to stick to her guns, but seeing Nanny Turner bustling round her cosy home, happily oblivious to the threat posed by Iris Langtry's friends, had made her rethink her position.

Iris herself was not too pleased with the bargain that had been struck, but accepted it grudgingly.

'Margot deserves a chance of happiness,' she sighed. 'And Steven is such a fine man. His wife's one of these very *domestic* women, I understand. He needs someone to work alongside him, and boost his political career.'

If that was how he saw Margot, it was little wonder the country was in such a hell of a state, Meg thought uncharitably, as she made her unwilling preparations for the trip. Certainly no one could ever have described her stepsister as 'domestic'. She could barely boil water.

One unexpected bonus was the acquisition of some new clothes, which Iris insisted on paying for.

'You're supposed to be my daughter,' she cut short Meg's protests. 'You can't go looking as if you've dressed at War on Want.'

The new hair colour, too, had been an unexpected success. Meg's own natural shade had been softened to a dark blonde, and subtly highlighted.

She was almost too busy to mourn properly over the closure of the bookshop where she'd worked for the past eighteen months, following the proprietor's retirement, or to worry about where she'd work once her French escapade was safely behind her. For the moment, she had enough problems to contend with.

To her surprise, her employer, Mr Otway, had nodded approvingly over her trip. 'Ah, the Languedoc. Land of the troubadours. And of the Cathars,' he added.

'Cathars?' Meg questioned.

'Religious sect in medieval times. Believed all life was basically evil, and a constant search for the light. Condemned, naturally, as heretics by the established church who launched the Albigensian Crusade against them.'

Mr Otway sniffed. 'Not just a holy war, of course. The whole of the Languedoc was made up of rich states, independent of the King of France. He hated Raymond of Toulouse, the greatest of the southern lords, envied him his wealth, and the beauty and culture of southern life. Decided to use the Cathars as an excuse to move against him, and grab his possessions, all in the name of religion.

'But you'll love the Languedoc,' he went on more cheerfully. 'It's a passionate land—a place of extreme contrasts. Warm laughter, and bitter tears. Faithful love and implacable hatred.' He paused. 'Fierce sun and violent storms. The full force of nature unleashed.' He grinned maliciously at the look of apprehension on Meg's face. 'It will do you good,' he said with severity. 'Shake you out of a rut you're far too young to occupy.'

'But I've been happy,' Meg protested.

'No, you've been content—a very different thing. But I guarantee, child, you won't be the same person when you return from the Languedoc.' He gave a dry chuckle. 'No, not the same person at all.' He patted her on the shoulder. 'I predict you'll never settle for mere contentment again. And drink "a beaker full of the warm south" for me,' he added.

'Warm south' was putting it mildly, Meg thought, as she sat in a traffic jam outside Toulouse airport, feeling the perspiration trickling down between her breasts.

The car she'd hired was like an oven already, and she was only at the start of her journey to Haut Arignac. She'd arrived in France two days earlier than she was actually expected, with the intention of doing some sightseeing before joining the De Brissot household as Madame's *dame de compagnie*.

It would also give her a chance to practise her French. She'd been the star pupil at school, and gone on to improve her fluency at evening classes. But there'd be no opportunity to try out her skill at the Château Haut Arignac, as Margaret de Brissot had been told during the preliminary correspondence that 'Margot' spoke no French.

'Quite useful really,' her stepsister had commented offhandedly when Meg protested at the arbitrary decision. 'If anyone asks awkward questions, you can just play dumb.'

'I don't want to play anything,' Meg said bitterly.

She felt wretchedly guilty about the charade she was undertaking. She was setting out to deceive an elderly, nearly blind woman, and for what? To further her stepsister's ruthless determination to break up her lover's marriage. And to hurt some unknown and presumably unsuspecting woman and her children along the way.

Even the knowledge that Nanny's occupancy of Brydons Cottage would be secure couldn't alleviate her profound misgivings about the whole affair, and her unwilling role in it. Damn Margot and her sordid affair, she thought, drumming her fingers on the steering-wheel.

Then, as if a drain had been unblocked somewhere, the traffic moved off, and Meg realised she was on her way. She proceeded with a certain amount of care, at first, accustoming herself to the unfamiliar road conditions, as well as the novelty of having a vehicle totally at her own disposal. But it didn't take her long to realise she was on good roads, with far less volume of traffic to contend with than in England, and she began to relax.

The sky above her was brilliant blue, but as she drove east she could see clouds building over the high ground in the far distance, fluffy and unthreatening at first, but increasing in mass and density with alarming suddenness.

By the time she stopped to buy food for lunch, the skies were a lowering grey, and she cast an anxious glance upwards as she made her way back to the car from the *alimentation*, with her baguette, sliced ham, demi-kilo of peaches and sedate bottle of mineral water.

She'd planned to have a picnic in some quiet spot. She'd deliberately chosen a route away from the main thoroughfares, so that she could travel at her own pace—discover, she hoped, the real France.

Now it looked as if she might be about to discover some real French weather as well, although it was still very warm, if not downright clammy, and those threatening clouds might yet blow over.

But as a smattering of rain hit the windscreen she decided reluctantly to shelve her plans for an alfresco meal, and concentrate on finding somewhere to stay that night. A helpful girl at the *syndicat d'initiative* in the last town she'd passed through had recommended a small *auberge* at the head of the Gorge du Beron, and even marked it on Meg's map.

She found herself following a winding road into a valley flanked by steep rocky banks which soon grew high enough to call themselves cliffs. The road ran alongside a river, relatively shallow, but flowing fast over its stony gravel bed. Presumably this was the Beron, at whose source she would find the *auberge.*

And the sooner the better, she thought with dismay, as more water arrived suddenly, descending like an impenetrable curtain from the sky, its arrival announced by a flash of lightning and a resoundingly ominous crack of thunder.

Meg swore under her breath, turning her windscreen-wipers full on, but it was wasted effort. They couldn't cope with the sheer force of the rain flinging itself at the car. And she dared not drive blind on such a tortuous road, she thought, applying her brakes and easing the car as close as possible to the side of the road where the rocky overhang seemed to offer a degree of shelter.

Who could have expected such a change in the weather? she wondered dispiritedly, although Mr Otway had warned her that these *orages* were common in the Languedoc, and it was safer to stay in one's vehicle than risk being struck by lightning.

She felt cold suddenly, and reached for a jacket from the rear seat, pulling it round her shoulders with a slight grimace. A glance at the river sent another chill through her. It was rising alarmingly rapidly, the gravel banks almost covered now, and the water lapping greedily at the side of the road itself, already awash in several places.

Not a good place to have stopped, after all, she realised in dismay. But she had to stay where she was now, until the rain eased a little at least. The storm was directly overhead now, thunder and lightning occurring almost simultaneously. Meg felt as if she was peering through a wall of water. Maybe it would have been better to have arrived on the appointed day, and been met at the airport as Madame de Brissot had originally suggested.

Or would it? That was the straightforward—the sensible course of action she'd been following for most of her life.

Don't be so boring, she chastised herself mentally. Where's your spirit of adventure? The car rocked suddenly as if caught in a violent gust of wind, and Meg shivered in spite of herself, then cried out in fear as her driver's door was wrenched open, filling the car with cold, sodden air.

For a dazed instant she thought the storm itself was responsible, then she saw the dark, caped figure framed in the doorway, staring in at her, and shrank back in her seat. She wanted to scream, but her vocal cords seemed paralysed with fright.

'Are you quite mad?' His voice was low-pitched, vibrant, and almost molten with rage. 'Do you want to be killed? Move this car now—at once.'

No spirit conjured up by the storm, but an all too human and angry male. He spoke in French and Meg replied automatically in the same language, her heart thumping violently in mingled alarm and relief.

'What gives you the right to order me about?'

'The right of someone who obviously knows this country better than you,' was the crushing retort. 'It isn't safe to park under a rockface in conditions like this, you little fool. There are often landslips. Your car could be buried, and you with it. So move. Quickly.'

However unpleasant he might be, he seemed to know what he was talking about, Meg realised uneasily. Perhaps she'd do well to accept his arrogant and unwelcome advice.

'Where do you suggest I park, then?' she asked, coldly.

'There is a safer place two hundred metres further on. Follow my car, and I will show you. And hurry,' he added grimly.

Her door slammed shut again, and he disappeared. A moment later, Meg saw the dim shape of a car overtake hers and halt some distance ahead of her, hazard lights blinking. Reluctantly, she turned the key in the ignition, but instead of the usual reassuring purr into life from the engine she was greeted with a profound and ominous silence.

Oh, no, Meg groaned inwardly, and tried again. And again. But the wretched engine stubbornly refused to fire.

'What's the matter now?' Her caped crusader, his temper apparently operating perfectly on all cylinders, reappeared beside her.

'What does it look like, you prat? The blasted car won't start,' Meg flung back at him in a savage undertone, while she searched for the appropriate and slightly more diplomatic phraseology in French.

'So you are English?' he remarked, switching effortlessly to her language. 'I should have guessed.'

His tone bit with contempt, and Meg stiffened in annoyance. Of course, he would have to be bilingual, she thought, feeling faint colour rise in her cheeks at the memory of her schoolgirl rudeness.

'What's the problem with the car?' he continued. 'Has it given trouble before?'

'It's hardly had the chance,' she said wearily. 'I only rented it today. But now the engine's dead. I suppose some water's got into the plugs, or the carburettor.'

He muttered something under his breath which Meg chose not to hear.

'Leave it here, then,' he ordered peremptorily, raising his voice above the crashing of the rain, 'and come with me.'

'I can't just abandon the thing,' Meg protested. 'It doesn't belong to me. And besides . . .' she hesitated '. . . I don't know you from Adam.'

'Sit here much longer, *mademoiselle*, and you may make the acquaintance of the original Adam— in Paradise.' His tone was caustic. 'You have more to fear, I promise, by remaining where you are than from accepting my assistance, such as it is.'

He paused. 'And rape, be assured, is the last thing on my mind in these conditions. Now get out of the car before we both drown.'

Meg obeyed unwillingly, flinching as the water soaked up through the thin soles of her sandals. Reaching his car was going to be like fording the river itself. She'd be drenched before she'd gone a couple of metres. She wondered glumly what Madame de Brissot's reaction would be if her new companion arrived at Haut Arignac with double pneumonia.

There was a swift impatient sigh beside her, and she found herself suddenly enveloped in his cape, held with disturbing force against his body under its voluminous folds, as she was half led, half carried to the other vehicle. Her nostrils were assailed by a tingling aroma of warm, clean wool, coupled with the individual and very masculine scent of his skin. She was aware too of the tang of some expensive cologne.

'Thank you,' she gasped with irony, as she was thrust without particular ceremony into the passenger seat.

'*Pas du tout*,' he returned. 'Now let's get out of here. It's always been a danger spot.'

Even as he spoke, Meg heard a sound like a low groan, followed by a strange rushing noise. She craned her neck, staring back down the gorge, and saw, with horrified disbelief, a tree come sliding down, roots first, from the heights above, and land with a sickening crash on the roof of her little Renault. It was followed by a deluge of earth and stones, bouncing off the bodywork on to the road, like a series of miniature explosions. A few even reached the other car, where they both sat stunned and immobile.

The silence which followed was deafening by comparison. And, as if finally satisfied with its efforts, the rain began to ease off.

CHAPTER TWO

MEG'S companion was the first to move, to break the profound hush.

He said quietly, '*Et voilà*,' and shrugged.

'Oh, God,' Meg breathed almost inaudibly. 'Oh, dear God.'

The driver's side had sustained the most damage, she realised numbly. The crumpled roof was practically resting on the seat, and the windscreen had been shattered by a large branch.

And up to a moment ago she'd been sitting there—right there. If he hadn't come along when he did—made her get out... Her mind closed off in shock, refusing to contemplate the undoubted consequences. She tried to speak—to thank him properly this time, and instead, to her shame, burst into tears.

He muttered something else under his breath, then swung into the seat beside her, flinging the discarded cape into the back of the car, before reaching into the glove compartment for a packet of tissues and a silver flask.

'Here,' he said curtly, unscrewing the flask's stopper. 'Drink this.'

It was cognac. She gasped, and choked, feeling the spirit spread like fire through her cold and shaking body. She dabbed at her face with a tissue. 'My car,' she whispered. 'My car.'

'You insured the car when you hired it,' he reminded her. 'It can easily be replaced. But not so your life.'

'No.' She shuddered uncontrollably, then lifted the flask again, taking a fierce, searing swallow, fighting back the remaining tears, and feeling the trembling dissipate slowly.

'I think you have had enough.' There was a faint smile in his voice as he gently detached the flask from her grasp.

When she was sure she was in control of her voice, she said, 'All—all my things were in the boot. I—I know it's silly to mind...'

'I'll get them.' He took the Renault's keys from her unresisting fingers.

'No.' Meg grabbed at his arm. 'Leave them, please. Don't risk it...'

'It's all right.' His voice was gentler. He pointed back towards the wreck. 'See, the boot was hardly touched.'

'But there might be another landslide.' There were still lightning flashes in the overcast sky, and thunder was grumbling around in the distance like some outraged but unseen giant. Meg could visualise more rocks, raining down on him, crushing him like the Renault.

She found she was looking at him, seeing him properly for the first time in the sullen light which penetrated the car. She knew that he was tall, and she'd had first-hand experience of the whipcord strength of his body during that headlong dash from the Renault, but that was the extent of it. Now she saw that he was quite young—not more than the early thirties at a guess, although she was no judge of such things. She assimilated a mass of unruly black hair, and a thin olive-skinned face, the lines of nose, mouth and chin strongly, even arrogantly marked. And dark fathomless eyes under heavy lids.

'I think the worst is past.' He shrugged again. He slanted a smile at her. 'Besides, I lead a charmed life.'

She could believe it. Nevertheless, she sat rigidly, staring ahead of her, not daring to look back, waiting for the clatter of falling stones and the cry of agony which seemed inevitable. But there was nothing but the rush of the water in the swollen river, and somewhere near by the shrill song of a bird announcing that the storm was over.

It occurred to her that he was taking a long time. She turned her head, peering back, and saw him standing at the rear of the Renault, very still, as if he'd been turned into a rock or a tree himself.

Maybe the boot was jammed, and he couldn't open it, she thought. But it seemed she was wrong, because almost at once he headed back towards the Citroën he was driving, striding out with a travel bag in each hand. She heard them thud as he transferred them to his own boot.

When he rejoined her, he looked preoccupied, his brows drawn together in a frown. She sensed a tension in him that she'd not been aware of before, as if he was angry about something, and trying to hide it.

Perhaps he'd only just realised that his act of gallantry had saddled him temporarily, at least, with an unwanted passenger, Meg thought with a certain compunction. Well, she could hardly blame him for resenting the disruption of his journey. Now it was her turn to reassure him.

She drew a careful breath. 'You've been very kind,' she said, 'and I hate to impose on you further, but I do need a lift to the Auberge du Source du Beron. I can get a room there—arrange something about the car too, with any luck.'

He seemed deep in thought, but at her words he turned his head and looked at her.

'You have a reservation at the *auberge*?' He sounded surprised.

'Well, no,' she admitted. 'But it's where I was heading before the storm. It's been recommended to me.'

'It's very popular with tourists. You'd have done well to book in advance, I think.' His frown deepened. 'You have no alternative plan?'

'Nothing definite,' Meg returned. She could hardly ask him to drive her all the way to Haut Arignac, she thought. The accident had been a severe set-back, admittedly, but she was still reluctant to arrive at the château a minute before she had to. She summoned up a ghost of a smile. 'I'll just have to risk there being a room.'

He gave her another long look. He said softly, 'It is not always wise, *mademoiselle*, to take risks—so far away from home.'

There was an odd note in his voice, an undertone of warning—even menace, she thought, a faint *frisson* of alarm uncurling down the length of her spine. Or was it just the shock she'd suffered playing tricks with her imagination?

It had to be that, because suddenly he smiled at her, charm softening the autocratic firmness of his mouth, and dancing in his eyes.

He wasn't exactly handsome, Meg thought, blinking under the onslaught, but, dear God, he

was frighteningly attractive. The kind of man she'd
never thought to meet. And she would be so glad to
get to the *auberge* and see the last of him, because,
the spirit of adventure notwithstanding, some un-
suspected female instinct told her that this man
represented more danger than any landslide she
might encounter.

She saw his smile twist slightly, as if he'd guessed
the tenor of her thoughts, and was amused by them.
He said softly, '*En avant*. Let's go.' And started the
car.

It was not a pleasant journey, although it had
stopped raining and the storm had rumbled its way
into some far distance, allowing a watery sun to
make an apologetic appearance.

Her companion was quiet, Meg found, if not
positively taciturn, but that was probably because
he had to concentrate so hard on driving. It was
perilous stuff. The road was littered with fallen de-
bris, and several times they even had to stop the car
to move rocks and tree branches which were actually blocking the road.

'Is it always as bad as this?' she asked, as he came
back to the car, dusting his hands on his jeans.

'I have known worse.' He glanced sideways at her
as he restarted the car. 'It has been alarming, your
introduction to France?'

'How did you know that? That it's my first time here?' Meg pulled a face. 'From my bad French, I suppose.'

He shrugged. 'It was just a guess. I didn't know it at all. And your French is very good,' he added drily. 'Remarkably so.'

'Why do you say that?'

'Because so many of your countrymen do not bother with our language,' he said, after a slight pause. 'They assume that if they shout loudly enough and slowly enough we will understand them.'

Meg gave a rueful nod. She'd heard much the same from her night-school teacher, a French-woman married to a Brit. 'I think it's to do with being an island race, and not feeling part of Europe. Maybe things will improve once the Channel Tunnel is open.'

'Perhaps.'

There was a further silence. He drove well, Meg thought, using the powerful capacity of the car without flourish, the lean brown hands in effortless control of the wheel.

He was simply dressed, but his denim jeans bore a designer label, and the plain white shirt, its cuffs turned back to reveal sinewy forearms, had an expensive silky sheen. His only adornment was a classic gold wristwatch with a brown leather strap.

It was difficult to know what to make of him, Meg thought, observing him under her lashes. He didn't slot into any obvious category, either social or professional. But then, she was no expert, she reminded herself wrily. Her experience of men was minimal, unless you counted Mr Otway, or Tim Hansby who collected books on military history, and who'd invited her once to London with him, on a visit to the Imperial War Museum.

Meg had enjoyed the museum more than she'd anticipated, but Tim, devoted only son of a widowed mother, would never be more than a casual friend. He still lived at home, and Meg pitied any girl who might fall in love with him, because Mrs Hansby was grimly determined to preserve the status quo.

Whereas her companion today didn't look as if he could be tied to any woman's apron strings. But appearances could be deceptive. He might well have a shrewd-eyed wife, and a brood of children, and tonight, over dinner, he'd tell them how he'd rescued a lone English tourist from the storm, making it amusing—minimising their narrow escape.

And later, his wife would ask when they were alone, 'What was she like—this English girl?' and he'd smile and say,

'Ordinary—I barely noticed her...'

As he glanced towards her, Meg realised she'd allowed a tiny sigh to escape her, and hurried into speech.

'Is it much further to the *auberge*?'

'About a kilometre. Do you find the journey tedious?'

'Oh, no,' she denied hurriedly. 'But I realise that you must have things to do—other plans. I feel I'm being a nuisance.'

'You are wrong. It is my pleasure to do this for you. Besides, by taking this road, I pass the *auberge* anyway, so it works out well for us both.' He paused again. 'My name is Jerome Moncourt,' he added with a touch of formality. 'May I know yours in return?'

Her lips parted to say Meg Langtry, but she hesitated, the words unspoken. She'd come here to be Margot, after all, she thought guiltily, and she'd almost forgotten. But, she supposed, the deception had to start somewhere. So why not practise her new identity on this stranger? After all, she was never going to see him again. Yet, at the same time, she was reluctant to tell a downright lie. I'm not the stuff conspirators are made from, she thought with a stifled sigh.

She forced a smile. 'Let's just say—Marguerite,' she temporised. It was a half-truth, after all, and, with luck, it might be all she'd need.

'The name of a flower,' he said softly. 'And of a famous French queen. You've heard, perhaps of La Reine Margot who was born Marguerite de Valois and married Henri of Navarre? She held court at Nerac in Gascony, and was one of the famous beauties of her age. She was what they used to call *une dame galante*.'

'Meaning?' Meg had moved with slight restiveness when she heard the name. Margot, she thought. Of course, it would be. She couldn't get away from it.

Jerome Moncourt shrugged again. 'That she enjoyed adventures—particularly with men other than her husband,' he returned. 'Her *affaires* were notorious.'

'Then she couldn't have been very happy with this Henri of Navarre.'

He laughed. 'Oh, he was not faultless, either. Maybe that is why he is one of the kings that France remembers with affection. *Un vrai brave homme*.'

'And of course in those days all marriages were arranged,' Meg said thoughtfully. 'I suppose they could be forgiven for straying if they were tied to someone they didn't care about.'

'But what if the marriage had been for this thing we call love?' His voice was cynical.

'Then there'd have been no excuse,' Meg said firmly.

'I am surprised to hear you say so.'

'Why?' Meg found herself bristling slightly.

Jerome Moncourt hesitated momentarily, then lifted a shoulder. 'Oh—because that is no longer a fashionable point of view. Easy marriage, easy divorce. That is the modern creed.'

Meg shook her head. 'I don't believe that,' she said. 'Divorce is never easy. Someone's always hurt—left behind, especially when there are children.'

He flicked her a swift sideways glance. 'I did not expect to meet with an idealist.'

'But then,' Meg said sedately, 'you didn't expect to meet me at all.'

'No?' He was smiling again. She felt his charm touch her like a caressing hand. 'You don't think it was fate rather than the storm which brought us together?'

Meg, uneasily aware of an unfamiliar trembling in the pit of her stomach, managed a laugh. 'I'm English, *monsieur*. I tend to blame the weather for everything.'

He laughed too. 'And in France, *mademoiselle*, we say that the marguerite always turns to the sun. Remember that.' He paused. 'And there just ahead of us is the *auberge*.'

A sudden surge of disappointment rose up inside her, and was ruthlessly crushed. Was she out of her mind, letting a complete stranger get to her like this? He'd rescued her, and she'd always be grateful for that, but she wasn't even sure she liked him, for heaven's sake. He was an unknown quantity, and she had enough problems ahead of her without taking him into the reckoning.

It was probably second nature to him to flirt with every girl he came across, she thought. She just wasn't used to his kind of man, or any other for that matter.

The Auberge du Source du Beron was a comfortable rambling building, probably a converted farmhouse, set at the rear of an enclosed courtyard.

Jerome Moncourt drove under an arched gateway into the courtyard, and stopped. Meg straightened her shoulders, and held out a hand, with a determined smile. 'Well, thank you again, and goodbye.'

'You are very eager to be rid of me,' he commented, his mouth twisting sardonically.

'Oh, it's not that,' she said hurriedly. 'But I've taken up too much of your time already.'

'You must allow me to judge for myself.' Jerome Moncourt left the car, and walked round to the passenger door to assist Meg to alight. 'Go and see if they have a room,' he directed, smiling faintly. 'I will bring your cases.'

Wide glass doors flanked by tubs of brilliant flowers opened on to a tiled reception area, where the *patronne* gave Meg a pleasant if harassed welcome.

Yes, there was a room, which she would be happy to show *mademoiselle*, but there was also a problem. Because of that devil's storm, there was no electricity. Until the supply could be restored, there would only be lamps or candles. As for the dining-room—*madame* made a gesture of despair.

'That doesn't matter,' Jerome Moncourt said over Meg's shoulder. '*Mademoiselle* is dining with me.'

Meg felt sudden swift colour invade her face, as *madame*, putting her troubles aside for a moment, lifted her eyebrows in a roguish and wholly approving assessment of the situation in general and Jerome Moncourt in particular. She then became brisk again. If *monsieur* would be so good as to transport the luggage to *mademoiselle's* room— Millot, whose task this was, being totally engaged in filling lamps—she would be forever grateful.

'*D'accord*.' Jerome smiled at her. 'But first I must ask if the storm spared the telephone. We need to report an accident.'

The phone system apparently was in full working order. Jerome lifted an eyebrow at Meg. 'Do you wish me to contact the authorities—deal with the formalities for you? It would perhaps be easier, no matter how good your French . . .'

Meg said a shy 'Thank you' and allowed *madame* to conduct her up the wide wooden staircase to a room at the back. The ceiling was low, and the floor uneven, but the furniture gleamed with polish, and the wide bed was made up with snowy linen and a duvet like a drift of thistledown. In one corner, a door opened on to an immaculate shower-room hardly bigger than a cupboard.

The small square window set deep in the thick stone wall stood open to admit the return of the sun, and the air, still cool after the rain, was heavy with the scent of lavender. Meg drew one deep enraptured breath. *Madame* gave a satisfied nod, and returned to her duties downstairs, closing the door behind her.

Meg stayed at the window. It had been quite a day, and it wasn't over yet—unless, of course, she wanted it to be. And she wasn't sure how she felt about that.

Things like this don't happen to me, she thought with bewilderment. But then I'm not myself any more. I'm supposed to be Margot. Perhaps I've taken over her life as well as her name. But can I carry it off?

She heard the door open, and Jerome enter with her luggage. Her heart began to thud, and her mouth went dry.

'Another car will be delivered to you in the morning,' he said, hoisting her cases on to the slatted wooden rack provided for the purpose. 'You will have to complete an accident report, but you have me as a witness, so there should be no difficulty.'

She kept her back towards him, moistening her lips with the tip of her tongue. 'I—I'm very grateful.'

'Grateful enough to be my guest at dinner tonight?' He was standing behind her, so close that she could feel the warmth from his body.

She stared at the view as if she was trying to memorise it. Behind the *auberge*'s small walled garden, the ground rose sharply. It was a wild and rocky landscape, studded with clumps of trees. A stream, presumably from some underground spring, had forced itself between two of the largest boulders, splashing down in a miniature waterfall, its passage marked by the sombre green of ferns.

'The source of the Beron,' Jerome said at her shoulder. She nodded jerkily, and after a pause he said, 'You do not, of course, have to accept my invitation.'

She knew that. Knew, too, that it would be safer—much safer to refuse politely, and, with sudden exhilaration, that she had no such intention.

As she turned to answer him, she caught a glimpse of his reflection in one of the windowpanes, his face dark and watchful, his mouth grimly set. She gasped, and her head came round sharply. But it must have been some trick of the light, because he looked back at her casually, even with faint amusement.

He said softly, 'Put me out of my misery, Marguerite. May I return for you here at eight?'

She said, 'Yes—I'd like that.'

And wondered, once she was alone, whether that was really true.

CHAPTER THREE

MEG took a long, luxurious shower, then spent some considerable time deciding what to wear that evening. In the end she fixed on a simple honey-coloured cotton dress in a full-skirted wrap-around style. She fastened gold hoops into her ears, and sprayed on some of her favourite Nina Ricci scent.

She studied her appearance frowningly in the cheval mirror, from the shining tumble of hair, framing a slightly flushed face, and hazel eyes strangely wider and brighter than usual, down to her slender feet in the strappy bronze sandals, then shook her head.

I feel like the old woman in the nursery rhyme, she thought—'Lawks-a-mercy, this be none of I.'

It was daunting to realise that if Jerome Moncourt had come strolling into Mr Otway's bookshop during the past eighteen months he probably wouldn't have given her a second look. She still wasn't sure why she'd agreed to have dinner with him. It wasn't the wisest move she'd ever made. After all, she knew nothing about him but his name, and that could well be an invention.

Oh, stop being paranoid, she admonished herself impatiently. Just because you're playing a part, it doesn't mean everyone else is too. And she could not deny that he'd fallen over himself to be helpful, but there could well be another side to him, she thought, remembering that unnerving, frozen glimpse she'd caught of his reflection, and that other moment, earlier in the day, when she'd felt his anger in the car reach out to her like a tangible thing.

Perhaps he was one of those people whose moods changed in seconds, or, more likely, maybe she was just imagining things. I just don't know any more, she thought, turning away from the mirror. But the invitation had been made in *madame*'s presence which seemed to suggest it was above-board. And at least she wouldn't dine alone on her first evening in the Languedoc. She felt a swift glow of excitement.

She caught up her bag, and the book on the history of the Cathars that Mr Otway had given her on parting, and went downstairs to wait for him. In Reception, *madame* was conducting a full-blooded argument by telephone, illustrated by gestures, with some hapless representative of the electricity company, but she smiled at Meg and motioned her to go through to the courtyard.

The sun was back in full force, bathing the whole area in syrupy golden light, and Meg sat at one of the small wrought-iron tables which had been placed outside, sipping a *pastis*, and reading.

It was difficult to comprehend on this beautiful evening, and rather depressing too, that the Cathars had believed the world to be the devil's creation, and man and all his works intrinsically evil. To escape damnation they had pursued a strict regime of prayer and abstinence, including vegetarianism, and the leaders of the cult, known as the Perfect Ones, also advocated celibacy in marriage.

Presumably the majority of their followers had decided to be not quite so perfect, otherwise Catharism would have died out in a generation, Meg thought.

From a modern viewpoint, their creed seemed eccentric rather than dangerous, yet armies had been sent to wipe them off the face of the earth. A bit like taking a sledgehammer to swat a fly.

Probably, as Mr Otway had said, it was greed for the riches of the South which had sent the Crusaders south, ravaging the vineyards and looting the cities, and religion was just the excuse.

She knew, before his shadow fell across the open page, that Jerome had arrived. She'd become aware of the stir at the adjoining tables, of the raised eyebrows and murmured asides as women turned their heads to watch him cross the courtyard.

'*Bonsoir.*' This evening, he was wearing well-cut cream trousers and a chestnut-brown shirt, open at the neck, while the mane of dark hair had been controlled, but not tamed.

Perhaps that was a clue to his personality, she found herself thinking as she shyly returned his smile of greeting. That under the expensive clothes and civilised manners there was a streak of wildness, waiting to explode. She wondered if he was an artist, perhaps. If so, he was a very successful one. The watch, the car, everything about him spelled out serious money.

If he'd noticed the interest his arrival had caused, he gave no sign of it, as he pulled out a chair and sat down, signalling to the hovering waiter to bring him a drink. She approved of his seeming unawareness of his own attraction. And he wasn't just attractive, either, Meg acknowledged wrily. For the first time in her life, she'd encountered a man who possessed a powerful sexual charisma that transcended ordinary good looks, and she wasn't sure how to deal with it.

'You looked very serious just now,' he observed, adding water to his *pastis*. 'You are not suffering from delayed shock, I hope?'

Meg shook her head, wrinkling her nose slightly. 'Actually I was thinking about man's inhumanity to man.'

'A sad thought for such an evening.' He glanced at her book, his brows lifting. *'Land of the Cathars,'* he read aloud. 'You are interested in the history of the Languedoc?' he asked, sounding genuinely surprised.

'Why not?' Meg lifted her chin. Just because she'd delayed leaving her car at his command, it didn't make her a complete idiot, she thought crossly.

He looked at her for a long moment, the expression in the dark eyes unreadable, then he shrugged. 'As you say—why not?' he agreed. 'You are a creature of surprises, Marguerite.'

'Not just me,' she reminded him, feeling oddly defensive. 'Neither of us knows the least thing about the other.'

'So tonight,' he said softly, 'will be a journey of discovery, *hein*?'

She bit her lip. That had altogether too intimate a ring, she thought uneasily. And his dark gaze had begun its journey already, travelling in silent appraisal down from her face to the rounded curves of her breasts under the cling of the cross-over bodice.

Meg, about to draw a deep, indignant breath, checked the impulse. It would have totally the wrong effect in the circumstances, she told herself tersely. Perhaps Monsieur Moncourt was completely *au fait* with the effect he had on women, after all, she thought with angry derision, and was confident of an easy seduction. Payment, maybe, for helping her out. Well, don't count on a thing, she assured him in grim silence.

This was the kind of game that Margot would enjoy, she realised. A sophisticated advance and retreat, spiced with unspoken promise and sexual innuendo, from which at the end she would walk away. Or not, as she chose.

And perhaps, just for one evening, it would do no harm to play the game herself—or at least learn some of its rules. Maybe this is my day for living dangerously, she thought.

Jerome Moncourt finished his drink and glanced at her empty glass. 'Shall we go?' he said. 'I hope your adventure today has given you an appetite?'

'My first experience of French cooking.' Meg smiled brightly as she pushed her chair back. 'I can't wait.'

The sun was beginning to set in a blaze of crimson as they drove out of the valley.

'Oh, how wonderful.' Meg craned her neck. 'It's going to be a fine day tomorrow.'

He smiled. 'No more storms,' he said teasingly, and she shuddered.

'I hope not.'

'You were unlucky,' he said. 'It is more usual for the storms to come at night. Sometimes as you drive you see the lightning playing round the hills, like a gigantic silent spotlight. We call it the *éclairs de chaleur*. Then suddenly a fork will streak to the ground, and the world goes mad. As you saw.'

'I did,' she said ruefully. 'Don't you have any gentler form of *son et lumière* for the tourists?'

'Perhaps the dawn would suit you better,' he said. 'That trace of pure clear light in the sky that drowns the stars, before the sun even lifts its head over the horizon.'

'You sound like a poet,' Meg said, stealing a sideways glance. 'Is that what you are?'

He laughed. 'No, I regret, nothing so romantic, although my grandfather was deeply interested in the poetry of the region—the songs of the troubadours and those that followed.'

'Did he write himself?'

Jerome shook his head. 'He lived on the land in a *mas* which belonged to his family. Grew his own vines. Adopted the simple life.'

'It sounds—good.'

'I think it was, for a time. Unhappily, even the simple life can become complicated, and eventually he returned to Paris.'

'And do you—lead the simple life too?'

'When I can.' He slanted a smile at her. 'But most of the time I'm an architect. I used to work in Paris, but our business expanded quite remarkably, and now I am based in Toulouse.'

'Back to your roots.'

'As you say. I work mainly as a consultant, advising on the preservation and restoration of old buildings—houses, usually, which have been allowed to become derelict during the drift from the land to the cities, but which are now in demand again.'

'Actually, I think that's quite as romantic as poetry,' Meg said thoughtfully. 'Repairing the fabric of history.'

His smile widened. 'And actually I agree with you, but I don't tell my clients, or they would expect me to work for love and not for money.'

'Are you working on a project at the moment?'

'In a way, although I'm officially on leave.' He didn't seem to want to enlarge on the subject, so Meg left it there.

'Do you miss Paris?' she asked, after a pause.

He shook his head. 'I wouldn't miss any city,' he said flatly. 'My family chose to live there. I did not.'

'Were they from this part of the country originally?'

'Yes. Our roots have always been here. My grandfather was the first to move away completely, in fact.'

'Was he never tempted to return?'

Jerome shrugged. 'My grandmother was a Parisienne,' he said tonelessly. 'She had no taste for the country.'

'But you've come back.'

'Yes,' he said. 'To the country of my heart. The place where I belong.'

It must be good to have such certainty, Meg thought rather wistfully. She wasn't sure where she stood in the scheme of things. She still lived at her late father's house, but it had been totally transformed to Iris Langtry's taste, and Meg felt like an outsider there most of the time. And she no longer had a job to hold her. So, she supposed, the world was her oyster now. Maybe it was time she found where she belonged. Put down some roots of her own.

In the meantime, she was beginning to wonder where they were going. She'd presumed he was taking her to some local restaurant where the electricity was still functioning, but they were still travelling purposefully, the Citroën eating up the kilometres. She wished she'd been watching the signposts, so that she could have followed their route on the map she had in her bag.

'You would like some music?' He seemed to have noticed her slight restiveness.

'No,' she denied quickly. 'I like to watch the scenery, and talk. But you must stop me if I ask too many questions.'

'You're unlikely to ask anything I won't wish to answer.' The dark eyes flickered towards her, then returned to the road. 'Can you say the same, Marguerite?'

'Of course,' she said stoutly, crossing her fingers metaphorically. 'I've nothing to hide.'

'A woman without secrets,' he said musingly. 'Unbelievable.'

She laughed. 'No, I just lead an uncomplicated and rather boring life.' Or I did, she thought.

'Yet you travel alone through choice, and have a deeper interest in this region than the average tourist. That is hardly dull. I think you have hidden depths, Marguerite.'

There was a note in his voice which made her heart leap in sudden ridiculous excitement. She said rather breathlessly, 'But then they say that everyone's more interesting on holiday.' There was a brief silence.

'Tell me,' he said softly, 'why you were so reluctant to answer when I asked you to dine with me?

There is a man in England, perhaps, who might cause—complications?'

Meg stared ahead of her. Tim Hansby? she thought with a kind of desperate amusement. She said shortly, 'There's no one.'

'*Vraiment*?' Jerome Moncourt sounded sceptical. 'I cannot believe there is no one you care about.'

She shrugged, pride making her reluctant to admit that up to now she'd occupied a fairly undistinguished place on the shelf—that there were only two people she really cared about, she realised with a pang. A retired second-hand bookseller, and the elderly woman who'd taken the place of her mother, and given her the affection and comfort that her father, dazed with grief at the loss of his young wife, had been unable to bestow. For whose sake she was here in the first place. She swallowed. Not a lot to show for her twenty years, she thought. Although this was not the time to start feeling sorry for herself.

And what the hell? she argued inwardly. It's nothing to do with him if I prevaricate a little. Although why she should wish to appear marginally more interesting than actual reality was something she didn't want to examine too closely, she thought, biting her lip.

'Does it make any difference?' she challenged. 'An invitation to dinner hardly constitutes a major breach of faith.'

She took a breath. 'For all I know, you could be married.'

'Would it matter if I was?' he tossed back at her.

That sounded like hedging. Her heart plummeted in a dismay as acute as it was absurd.

'I think it might matter a hell of a lot to your wife,' she said curtly.

'Then it is fortunate she does not yet exist.' There was a note of mockery in his voice, mingled with something else less easy to decipher.

'Fortunate for her, anyway,' she muttered, self-disgust at the relief flooding over her making her churlish.

He clicked his tongue reprovingly. 'That's not kind. You don't think I'd make a good husband?'

'I can't possibly tell on so brief an acquaintance.' Meg kept her tone short. She knew he was laughing at her, even though his expression was serious, almost frowning.

'But you have an ideal? What qualities should he possess? Would you require him to be faithful?'

Meg twisted the strap of her bag in her fingers. 'I'd want him to love me, and only me, as I'd love him,' she said at last. 'I suppose that takes care of most things.'

'It is certainly sweeping,' Jerome said, after another pause. 'And if, in spite of that love, another woman intervened—tried to take this paragon away from you—what would you do then? Make the sacrifice? Let him go?'

'No,' she said, fiercely. 'I'd fight for him with everything I had.'

'You would be ruthless?' his voice probed softly. 'Use any weapon?'

'Of course.' She hesitated uncertainly. 'Why do you ask me all this?'

'Because I wish to know, *ma petite*,' he said softly. 'It is part of that journey of discovery I mentioned—to find that you would fight like a tigress for love.'

Again that odd note in his voice. Meg felt herself shiver. He noticed at once. 'You are cold?'

'Oh, no.' She forced a smile. 'Hungry, perhaps.' She thought of her picnic lunch, crushed in the car.

'You've been patient long enough. Now you shall be fed.' He turned the car suddenly off the road, and on to a track leading downhill. Meg braced herself as the Citroën swayed and jolted over stones and deep ruts.

'There's actually a restaurant down here?' she gasped. 'I hope there's another road out, or people's meals won't stay down for long.'

'Not a restaurant.' Ahead of them, bathed rose-pink in the sunset, there was a straggle of buildings, a chimney from which smoke uncoiled lazily in the still evening air.

'Then where are we?' They seemed to be in the middle of nowhere, she realised with alarm. And isolated too. There were no other cars around that she could see, so it couldn't be a very popular establishment.

'This is my house.' The mockery was back, full force. 'The family *mas* I was telling you about.'

He paused. 'I decided, *ma belle*, that we would dine at home tonight. Enjoy our mutual discoveries in private.' He let that sink in, then added silkily, 'I hope you approve?'

CHAPTER FOUR

THE silence in the car was almost electric. Meg was rigid, her mouth dry.

How could she have been such a fool? she asked herself with agonised disbelief. She should have listened to her misgivings, but instead she'd trusted him—because he was the first attractive man to show any interest in her, she flayed herself savagely—and now here she was, in some kind of ghastly trap.

This is my house. Here, in the back of beyond, miles from anywhere—and she didn't even know where 'anywhere' was.

' "Will you walk into my parlour?" said the spider to the fly.' And she'd done exactly that. A nightmare coming true.

Her hands curled into fists in her lap.

She said, keeping her voice cool and even, 'I seem to have lost my appetite. Will you take me back to the *auberge*, please?'

There was a silence, then Jerome Moncourt shrugged, the dark eyes agleam with amusement, as if he knew exactly the thoughts and fears churning under her calm exterior.

'Of course—if that is what you prefer,' he agreed equably. 'But Berthe will be desolated if you do not at least taste her *cassoulet*.'

'Berthe?' she questioned.

'My housekeeper,' he said. 'She and her husband Octavien have lived here, looking after the house and the vines, since my grandfather left. Now they look after me.' He pointed towards the house. 'See?'

A man had emerged from the front entrance, and was standing hands on hips, watching them curiously. He was of medium height and stocky build, his face as brown and wrinkled as a walnut, the inevitable beret pulled on over his shock of white hair. He had bow legs, and a drooping moustache, and bore no resemblance to the kind of sinister henchman who'd collaborate in kidnap and rape, Meg decided, feeling suddenly oddly reassured.

'Will you risk my dining-table now?' Jerome Moncourt enquired courteously. 'Or shall we eat here, in the car?'

Put like that, it did sound ridiculous, Meg admitted to herself, as she got out of the car with all the dignity she could muster.

'All the same,' she said, as they walked towards the house, 'you should have told me we were coming here.'

'Perhaps I did not dare. You might have refused—and,' his voice gentled, 'I so much wanted to see you tonight.'

It was the perfect answer, she thought. Perhaps almost too perfect, as if this was a well-practised line, her head reminded her as her heart began to thud against her ribcage. But then she surely didn't think she was the first young woman to feel her pulses quicken and her body grow feverish with excitement at the smile in his eyes?

And she'd been stupid to think he'd ever need to resort to rape, or any kind of force, she told herself wrily. His tactics would be far more subtle, and just as dangerous in their way. He was still the spider, and she the fly, and she mustn't forget that.

But his web was a delight.

The house was built on two storeys, the roof tiled in faded terracotta, sloping gently down to the storage buildings which flanked it. Beneath the roof, the stone walls were washed the colour of rich cream, dark green shutters guarded the windows, and a golden climbing rose flung a triumphal arch over the square doorway.

The door led straight into the main room of the house, the ceiling low and dark-beamed, the floor flagged. At one end there was a large fireplace, its massive hearth empty now. On either side of it two battered leather sofas confronted each other. Opposite the entrance, glazed doors gave access to a courtyard bright with stone troughs filled with flowers. In the corner, a spiral staircase led to the upper floor.

At the other end of the room was a magnificent refectory table at which two places were laid, and six high-backed leather chairs. Apart from a well-filled bookcase, and a bureau overflowing with papers, there was no other furniture. The effect was uncluttered, but it also created a very masculine environment with few soft touches, Meg thought, as she looked around her.

'Is this the project you talked of?' she asked, catching sight of some timber and other building materials in a corner of the courtyard.

He nodded. 'One of them. I'd thought of extending down the side of the yard at the back, converting one of the barns. I wanted to provide myself with a place to work, and also some guest accommodation. But I've decided against that now. To provide the space I need would spoil the whole feel of the *mas.*'

'Do you entertain a good deal?' She tried to sound casual.

'At the moment, not at all. I've been too busy.'
He paused. 'My first task when I came back here
was to remodel the upper floor. I wanted to start on
the kitchen——' he pointed to an archway, through
which Meg could glimpse a scrubbed table and an
old-fashioned range '—but Berthe wouldn't allow
it.'

Meg sniffed appreciatively at the savoury gar-
licky aroma emanating from the other room. 'I
think most cooks prefer a familiar stove.'

Octavien had preceded them into the house. Now
he appeared in the kitchen door, frowning por-
tentously, his wife behind him peering over his
shoulder. Berthe was a head taller than her husband, gaunt in a shapeless flowered cotton dress.
Her hair, iron-grey streaked with silver, was pinned
in an uncompromising knot on top of her head, and
her face was unsmiling and suspicious as she openly
looked Meg over.

Meg heard Octavien mutter something that
sounded like, 'Another Englishwoman,' but she
might have mistaken the harsh *patois* he used. In
any case, it was no business of hers what national-
ity the other women were that Jerome had brought
here, she thought, lifting her chin, and she had no
doubt there'd been some, no matter what his work
schedule might be. Perhaps, unlike his staff, he had
a penchant for foreigners.

'The food will be a few moments yet. Would you like to see the rest of the *mas*?' Jerome asked.

'Yes, that would be fine.' Meg smiled at the unresponsive faces in the kitchen doorway. 'It all smells so wonderful,' she said in French.

But there was no softening. The couple turned and vanished back into their domain, with only the clatter of saucepans and china as a reminder of their presence, as Meg followed Jerome up the spiral staircase. It emerged on to a narrow landing lined with beautifully made wooden cupboards.

'It was a maze of tiny rooms, all opening out of each other,' Jerome said. 'Now there is just a storage-room and a new bathroom next to it.' He threw open a door on the other side of the landing. 'And the rest is mine.'

No frills here either, thought Meg, stepping into a room which occupied at least two-thirds of the available first-floor space. The whole rear wall seemed to be glass, allowing a panoramic view of the wooded slopes of the valley and the tall crags beyond.

At the far end, skylights had been let into the roof to maximise the light, and here Jerome had a working-table, a vast surface covered by plans and drawings. Apart from a tall chest of drawers, the only other piece of furniture was the bed—more than kingsize, with elaborately carved head and footboards, and a coverlet in shimmering black and gold brocade.

There was something barbaric about it, thought Meg, something which made the bed, quite deliberately, the focal-point of the room. A kind of personal statement, whose message she'd prefer to ignore.

She studiously transferred her gaze to that amazing view instead. 'It's breathtaking,' she said. 'I can understand why you had the wall made into a window.'

Jerome came to stand beside her. 'And there is another advantage. You see that tall peak?' He pointed to a jagged outline against the pale evening sky. 'That is almost due east. From my bed, I can watch the dawn break.' He paused. 'In the right company it can be an inspiration.'

To her fury, Meg felt her face warm at the image his words had evoked.

Jerome lifted a hand and stroked a finger gently, lingeringly down the curve of her flushed cheek. He said softly, half to himself, ' "*Oi deus, oi deus, de l'alba tan tost ve.*" '

'I—I don't understand.' Meg felt her breathing go ragged as the caressing hand found the lobe of her ear, and the sensitive column of her throat, then moved to fondle the nape of her neck under the soft mass of hair. She knew she ought to stop this right now—step back out of range—but something kept her rooted to the spot.

'It's a line from a troubadour, *ma belle*, an *aubade*, a song of dawn, lamenting the swift passage of his night with his beloved.' He leaned towards her, and murmured the translation, his lips almost brushing her ear, '"Ah, God, ah God, but the dawn comes soon."'

Meg's flush deepened. She tried to move, to resist the blatant persuasion of his caress, because his fingers were on her back now, following the supple length of her spine. Urging her, she realised, too late, towards him. And into his arms, pinned against his body.

Jerome bent and took her mouth with his, coolly and unhurriedly, almost questioningly.

At the first silky contact, Meg's eyes closed. She felt his lips move on hers, coaxing them apart, felt the sweet fire of his tongue against hers as she capitulated helplessly. Letting the kiss deepen. Letting her mind—her will—spin into oblivion, as he drained all the sweetness from her mouth.

Jerome Moncourt lifted his head, and little devils danced in his eyes as he looked down at her. She stared back at him dazedly, knowing that he was going to kiss her again, knowing that she should resist—now, this minute—break free from whatever thrall he was weaving around her...

Then from the bottom of the staircase they heard Berthe calling, '*Monsieur Jerome—vous êtes servi*,' and the spell was broken.

Jerome's smile was faintly crooked. 'One appetite at a time, *mignonne*.' He took her hand, and pressed a swift kiss into the palm, making her whole body shiver in delight—in shameful anticipation.

She was trembling inside, her head light, her legs oddly weak. As she went down the spiral stair, she stumbled slightly, and his hand caught her, steadied her.

'Take care,' he warned on a note of laughter, as if perfectly aware of the havoc he'd created. Which, of course, he was. He was a sophisticated man with a whole battery of sensual expertise at his command. And she was a total novice.

As her untutored response to his kiss must have told him, she reminded herself bleakly. He'll think I'm a piece of cake—a pushover, she thought, gripping the narrow rail until her knuckles turned white. She needed to hang on. She couldn't afford any more slips, she told herself, swallowing. She also needed some food. It had been a long time—a lifetime—since breakfast.

A good meal would put fresh heart into her. It would also allow her a breathing space to decide how to deal with this potentially disastrous situation.

Downstairs, Berthe was placing a steaming tureen on the table, with a platter of bread next to it. She indicated with a jerk of the head that Meg and Jerome should sit at the table, and began to ladle the smoooth creamy concoction into pottery bowls, one of which she dumped in front of Meg.

She'd had more graciously served food, Meg thought, with faint amusement, but she knew after just one mouthful that she couldn't fault the cooking. The soup was delicious with a delicate flavour she did not immediately recognise.

'*Tourain toulousain*,' Jerome told her when she enquired. 'Garlic soup. You like it?'

'It's fantastic,' she said honestly. 'Please tell Berthe so. I don't think she understands me.'

'I'm afraid she does,' There was a touch of wryness in his voice. 'Berthe, you understand, has held a long and privileged position in my family. Sometimes she and Octavien take advantage of this. You must excuse them.'

Maybe she could take advantage of it too, Meg thought; use Berthe's overt disapproval of her presence to make a strategic withdrawal at the right time.

The soup was cleared away and replaced by a rich, meaty terrine, accompanied by a tomato salad, rich with virgin olive oil and fresh basil.

'I thought you mentioned *cassoulet*?' Meg said wonderingly.

He smiled at her. 'That is still to come.' He poured her red wine from an unmarked bottle. 'From my own vines,' he said.

Meg was beginning to think she couldn't eat another mouthful when the *cassoulet* arrived, served in a big earthenware pot. It was a brown and bubbling mixture of haricot beans, sausage and minced bacon with garlic cooked in layers around a large joint of pork.

Yet somehow she managed to demolish the plateful Jerome handed her with yet more bread, although she regretfully declined a second helping. She also refused more of the full-bodied, and, she suspected, lethally potent wine.

The meal was rounded of with a tart, in which swirls of thinly sliced apple had been cooked under a light glaze.

'I don't think,' Meg said reverently as she put down her fork, 'that I shall ever move again.'

He laughed. 'Ah, but you will,' he said. 'You lack practice in eating, that's all.'

'By the end of my stay I shall be like a barrel.'

'That will depend on the length of your stay.'

Of course, he thought she was here for a conventional vacation only. She wondered what he would say if she told him she was staying for a month. Not that she planned to tell him.

Ships that pass in the night, she told herself resolutely, as coffee was placed on the table by the surly Berthe, who then withdrew.

Meg watched her go with mixed feelings.

'She and Octavien occupy quarters on the other side of the kitchen,' Jerome told her softly, interpreting her expression with infuriating accuracy. 'If you scream loudly enough, they will hear you.'

'Thank you,' she said shortly. 'That's—very reassuring.'

'On the other hand,' he said, 'you may not wish to scream.' The words, and their implication, seemed to linger in the air, and she felt that betraying colour steal into her face again.

Margot wouldn't have sat here blushing like an idiot, she berated herself. She'd have flung back an answer—amusing, provocative, the outcome of the evening already decided in her own mind.

And not the decision Meg herself had reached…

'Some cognac with your coffee?' His voice cut across her confused jumble of thought. 'It will be quite safe,' he added with a touch of derision as she hesitated. 'Alcohol is only used by the clumsy, or the uncaring, as a means of seeking a woman's compliance.'

Meg stared down into the dark swirl of coffee. 'Is that what you look for—compliance?' she asked in a low voice.

'Perhaps that is the wrong word.' He frowned slightly, the dark eyes fixed on hers, his voice low— almost mesmeric. 'When I make love to a woman, *ma belle*, I demand her full response—to know beyond doubt that she feels as I do—wants what I want. Passion must be shared, or it is worthless.'

There was a brief silence. In spite of herself, Meg was aware of her body's involuntary reaction to his words, could feel her nipples tautening with excitement against the clinging fabric of her dress— knew, dry-mouthed, that he could not fail to notice that either.

'I don't think passion on its own counts for much, anyway,' she countered with a touch of desperation. 'It should be part of something else— something deeper, and more lasting.'

'A very moral point of view.' His mouth twisted. 'And yet one has to start somewhere, and usually it is with the kind of physical enchantment that we discovered, just now, in my room. You don't deny that, I hope?' he added mockingly, his gaze lingering on the betraying thrust of her breasts.

'On the basis of just one kiss?' Meg managed to invest her tone with an inflexion of amused scorn worthy of Margot herself. 'Really, *monsieur*, you may be very attractive, as I'm sure you know already, but perhaps you might be overestimating your appeal.'

'You think so?' he asked, silkily. 'Well, one kiss is hardly grounds for judgement, as you say, so let us see...'

He rose from his chair, and came round the table to her in what seemed to be one lithe, totally predatory movement. Meg found herself lifted from her chair into his arms, and carried across the room to one of the sofas.

'Let go of me.' Meg struggled, pushing at his chest with frantic fists.

'Presently,' he said softly. 'When I have completed my experiment.' He sat down, holding her pinioned across his body, one hand twisted ruthlessly in her hair, making it impossible for her to move. There was no gentleness either, this time, in the lips which plundered hers. He seemed savagely determined on enforcing a response from her, to salve, she supposed breathlessly, his wounded pride. She'd made him angry, and this bruising, burning possession of her mouth was to be her punishment.

Well, she could fight that with her own rage at his assumption that she'd be another easy conquest— an apple ripe to drop from the tree into his careless, outstretched hand.

Damn him, she thought raggedly. Damn him to hell.

At last, with a groan, he tore his mouth from hers. 'Marguerite.' The word was almost a sigh. 'Ah, *Dieu*, this is not the way.'

He bent, tracing the swollen outline of her lips with the tip of his tongue, while his hand lifted to pull aside the concealing fold of the honey-coloured dress and cup one lace-covered breast in his lean fingers.

The sudden volte-face from aggression to beguiling and seductive tenderness sent Meg's head reeling. She found herself sinking into his embrace, cradled against the lean warmth of his body, letting her lips caress his in turn with shy invitation. He gave a soft groan of satisfaction, then lifted his head to watch her face as his thumb stroked the suddenly tumescent nipple, sending a sensation of mingled pain and delight shafting through her body, making her gasp helplessly and revealingly.

No one had ever warned her that desire could be like this, she thought dazedly. So swift and all-encompassing, making you deaf and blind to everything but the primitive urgings of your newly awakened body.

When his mouth returned to hers again, she welcomed his kiss with eagerness and anticipation, her lips parting involuntarily, her tongue moving against his in instinctive eroticism. She felt him loosen the bow at her waist which fastened her dress. She lay, quiescent, her eyes fixed on his face, as he parted the dress, pushing the edges aside so that he could look at her.

The fragile scraps of underwear were an enhancement of her nakedness rather than a covering for it, the dusky aureoles of her breasts clearly visible through the flimsy lace bra, and the white V of her briefs shadowed by the darker, silky triangle beneath.

Jerome drew a sharp breath. '*Tu es toute belle,*' he muttered unevenly, his caressing hand sliding from her breast to her thigh in one lingering gesture of possession and promise.

At his touch, her body melted, and she arched towards him in mute yearning, pleading for his tutelage in all the ways of love.

The sudden shrill of the telephone shattered the golden intimate silence which surrounded them with devastating effect. It was as if someone had actually physically intruded into the room. Shocked back to her senses, Meg pulled herself away from him and sat up, dragging her dress into place with shaking hands.

He reached for her again. '*Doucement,*' he said hoarsely. '*Sois tranquille.*'

'No,' she said. And, 'No,' again. 'You must answer it. Or Berthe will hear it, and come. Won't she?'

'Yes,' he conceded with husky reluctance. He got up, pushing back his dishevelled hair and walked to the bureau, snatching up the receiver. He said curtly, 'Moncourt,' and paused, his face freezing into blankness. '*C'est toi?*' His tone softened perceptibly. 'Yes, I came back this evening.' He listened for a moment. '*Ma chère*, I can't talk now. It's impossible.' His voice sank to a murmur. 'We'll speak tomorrow. Yes, I promise.'

The tenderness in his words seemed to cut into Meg like the lash of a whip. One minute she'd been half naked in his arms, she accused herself in self-disgust, on the brink of losing all self-respect—all control. Now she was hearing him talk to another woman—someone with whom he was clearly on inintimate terms. Someone he'd been prepared to betray—with her.

It brought home to her in the plainest possible terms how little she knew of him. And, more tellingly, the totally transient place she occupied in his life. A painful lesson, but one she'd needed to learn.

A one-night stand, she thought, wincing. That was what she'd have been—all she'd have been, and yet she'd nearly allowed it to happen. Had let herself be taken almost to the brink, and beyond. That was what she was going to ultimately remember to her shame—how easy she'd made it for him. How stupidly, naïvely willing she'd proved... She choked back a sob as she tried to refasten her dress, her fingers clumsy with haste.

Jerome said, 'Yes, very soon. You have my word. *À bientôt.*'

Back turned towards him, she heard the phone go down on its rest. Mastering her voice with a supreme effort, she said, 'You can call her back right away, because I'm leaving now. Is there a local taxi service I could use?'

He came to stand behind her. His arms wrapped her tightly. His mouth grazed the side of her throat. He said quietly, 'I am sorry. I wasn't expecting any calls this evening. No one was supposed to know I had returned.'

As if that made it better, she thought bitterly, freeing herself from his encircling arms. This other girl had probably been living for the moment—couldn't wait any longer.

She said lightly, 'You're clearly irresistible. I'll leave you to get on with your busy life, while I enjoy the rest of my vacation.'

Jerome caught her arm, turned her to face him. He said, 'It's not what you think. She's a friend—that's all.'

Meg shook her head. 'It's really no concern of mine,' she said, avoiding the dark intensity of his gaze. 'It's been a pleasant evening, but it's over, and I simply must get back to the *auberge*. I have to make an early start tomorrow.'

'Then don't leave at all.' His voice was husky. 'Stay here with me, Marguerite. Watch the dawn in my arms.'

For a moment, her mind saw the huge bed with its brocade cover lit by the first shimmer of daylight over the eastern hills, and her heart lurched in temptation and longing.

Oh, God, she thought, what's the matter with me?

'No.' She detached herself from his grasp with cool determination. 'I—I can't.'

'Why not?' he urged. 'When it's what we both want?'

'Because,' she said slowly, choosing her words with care, 'you would be a complication I don't need.' She tried to smile. 'The simple life, remember.'

'Oh, no, Marguerite.' He shook his head, his mouth twisting. 'With you, *ma belle*, nothing would ever be that simple.' His voice hardened. 'So why did you agree to dine with me tonight?'

Meg looked down at the floor. 'It was wrong of me, I know. I suppose I—I didn't want to be alone this evening. It's been an unnerving day. It's knocked me a little off-balance—made me behave in a way that's completely out of character.'

He laughed suddenly—an ugly sound in the shadowed room. '*Au contraire*, I think I have seen exactly what you are. But for that—inconvenient intervention you would be in bed with me now, *ma belle*. You know it, and I know it too. But go, if you must. Forgive me if I don't escort you in person.' He strode across the room to the kitchen and shouted, 'Octavien.'

After a brief, tingling pause, the older man appeared, wiping his mouth on the back of his hand. He gave Meg a hostile glare from beneath his shaggy eyebrows, then turned a questioning glance on his employer. Jerome took his car keys from his pocket and tossed them to him. '*Mademoiselle* is leaving,' he said curtly. 'Please drive her to the Auberge du Source du Beron.'

Octavien nodded imperturbably. He produced his crumpled beret, put it on his head, and went out to the car.

Meg picked up her bag and looked at Jerome. 'Can we say—goodbye?' she asked past the pain constricting her throat.

The dark face was unreadable. 'We will say *au revoir*,' he said quietly. 'Because this is only the

beginning.' He gave a harsh laugh. 'I have not finished with you yet.'

Meg's heart lurched. That, she thought, is what
you think. She walked to the door, holding her head
high, trying not to hurry. His voice followed her,
mockingly. 'Sleep well, *chérie*—if you can.'

Octavien did not even look at her as she got into
the car. He simply started the engine and sent the
Citroën bumping back up the track. Meg's hands
clenched in her lap. She still could barely believe
what had happened—or what she'd almost allowed to happen, she amended with forlorn bewilderment. She might have behaved like a fool, but
for a brief hour or so she'd been shown passion—
she'd known what it was to be desired.

Now it was gone—like a waking dream banished
by the cold light of day. And she should be glad—
grateful for her reprieve. But the ache deep inside
her told a different story.

She thought, 'Ah God, ah God, but the dawn
comes soon,' and could have wept with sheer des-
olation.

CHAPTER FIVE

MEG finished the last morsel of croissant, and re-filled her coffee-cup. She'd paid her bill, and Millot had brought her bags down to the reception area. All she needed was the hire car to arrive, and she could be on her way.

During the course of a long and restless night, she'd decided to abandon her sightseeing plans and go straight to Haut Arignac, and the seclusion it offered. Once there, she would keep her head down, sit out the month as she'd promised, and return to England, hopefully unscathed, at the end of it.

And there would be no more ill-advised attempts to adopt Margot's persona as well as her identity, she told herself, biting her lip. That was the road to disaster. She would just have to put the events of the past twenty-four hours out of her mind as best she could, although it wouldn't be easy.

The inexperienced girl who'd driven out of Toulouse had vanished forever. In her place was a woman, awoken for the first time to her own needs. But needs that wouldn't be satisfied by someone like Jerome Moncourt—a chance-met stranger with a well-practised line in seduction, and a coterie of other women, she told herself strongly. She deserved better than that. She wasn't Margot. She didn't want someone else's man.

But for all that positive thinking she'd found it impossible to forget about the girl who'd telephoned last night. Her unknown saviour, she thought with self-derision, and maybe that was why she couldn't get her out of her mind.

As for Jerome Moncourt—well, he was out of her life now, and no real harm done—except perhaps to his sexual pride. She'd found his reaction to her departure disturbing, even vaguely threatening. But perhaps he just wasn't used to rejection, she thought with a faint sigh. And she'd given out all the wrong signals, after all. I'm not the type for casual encounters, she told herself. For me there'd have to be commitment, on both sides. And Jerome Moncourt wasn't that kind of man. Although she'd never be able to figure out his attitude towards her if she tried till doomsday. Unlike Octavien, she thought ruefully, who hadn't uttered a word all the way back to the *auberge*. He could be listed as 'hostile'. It was only as she'd got out of the car that he'd broken his self-imposed silence.

'*Anglaise.*' His gruff voice had made the word sound like an insult. 'Go back where you belong, and leave us in peace.'

There was nothing she'd like more, she'd thought with an inward grimace, but she was committed now. There was no turning back.

'*Mademoiselle*?' The waiter appeared at her side. 'Your car is here.'

She smiled her thanks, swallowed the rest of her coffee, and walked out to Reception—stopping dead when she saw who was waiting for her in the foyer.

'*Bonjour*, Marguerite.' Jerome Moncourt's smile approved her slim cream skirt and matching sleeveless top. 'You are dressed for the weather. It's going to be a hot day.'

'What are you doing here?' she demanded hoarsely.

'Taking you to Haut Arignac.' He glanced at his watch. 'You said you wished to make an early start.'

'Yes.' Meg mastered her voice, with an effort. 'But not with you.'

'I did warn you last night we had not seen the last of each other,' he reminded her.

'I remember,' she said tersely. Something else occurred to her. 'And how do you know I'm going to Haut Arignac?'

'Because that was the address on your luggage.'

Of course, she thought, her heart sinking. She said, 'How clever. But that doesn't mean I'm prepared to accept a lift—or spend even another minute in your company. I intend to make my own way to Haut Arignac.'

'It's quite a distance,' he said musingly. 'Even as the crow flies.'

'But I'm not going by crow,' she said. 'I have a rented car. Due any moment.'

Jerome shook his head. 'No, *hélas*. I cancelled it.'

'You did what?' Meg's voice rose to a shriek. She was aware of heads beginning to turn in their direction from elsewhere in the foyer, of the *patronne*'s twinkling-eyed interest from the reception desk.

'I told them it would not be needed,' he said. 'You'll be required to complete an accident report, but that can be done at your convenience. They have a branch office in Albi,' he added.

'I don't care if they have one on the moon.' Meg was shaking with temper. 'You had no right—no right at all ...'

'Shall we discuss that on the way?' He put a hand under her arm, and escorted her firmly out of the *auberge*, and across the courtyard. 'Your godmother is expecting us in time for lunch.'

'Godmother?' She was just about to say, What godmother? but pulled herself up, with a gasp. 'How did you know that?'

'Because Madame de Brissot is a client of mine. I am planning an extensive programme of repairs at the château on her behalf. The project I told you about?' He paused, letting that sink in. 'She has spoken of you a great deal. In fact I was detailed to collect you at the airport tomorrow, but she was delighted to know that you'd be delivered to her, safe and sound, a day early.' He paused again. 'Besides, there can hardly be two Margot Trants.'

That's what you think, Meg told him silently.

She said slowly, 'Then you must have known— last night...' Her voice trailed away.

Jerome nodded. 'Who you were—what you were—and your destination. All from those neat labels.'

'And yet you said nothing.' And you weren't pleased either, she thought, remembering that frozen figure at the side of the road.

Jerome shrugged. 'It was more amusing to keep silent,' he retorted. 'To enjoy a random encounter, and see where it led.' He paused, allowing her to assimilate the faint edge in his voice. 'And you were not being completely frank either—Marguerite.'

She flushed. 'I'm not obliged to give my life history to a stranger,' she countered. 'Besides, I thought—I hoped that was it. That I'd never see you again.'

'Yet here we are,' he said softly. He opened the passenger door of the car with almost exaggerated courtesy. 'You should have listened to me last night.'

'Well, now it's your turn to listen—before I get into this car.' She gave him a clear, cold look. It was another denim day, she noticed sourly, the beautifully cut jeans clinging to his lean hips and long legs. The blue cotton shirt was partly unbuttoned, revealing the bronzed, hair-darkened wall of his chest. She felt her throat tighten, and was aware, with shock, of a sudden moist warmth invading her body.

She swallowed. 'As far as I'm concerned, yesterday is over. In fact, it never happened. I'm here to work. To be Madame de Brissot's companion. And I don't want...' She hesitated.

'Complications?' he supplied softly.

'Precisely,' she said tautly. 'You do your job, I'll do mine. We'll leave it like that.'

'Maybe that isn't what I want.' His eyes skimmed her body, lingering on the curve of her breast under the clinging top, the slender line of her thighs under the brief skirt. His gaze seemed to touch her like a caressing hand, reminding her with nerve-shattering potency how, only a few hours before, she'd lain half naked and wholly vulnerable in his arms. And for one perilous moment the precision of that memory lit a small flame of response deep inside her. Exactly, she realised with dismay, as he'd intended.

She doused it instantly with anger. 'No?' Her eyes flashed. 'Then that's tough, *monsieur*, because I'm sure my godmother wouldn't want me being harassed in any way. In fact, if I informed her of your recent behaviour, she might even feel inclined to hire another architect,' she added coldly.

Jerome laughed. 'Threatening me, *ma belle*? I don't advise it. And I am not just at Haut Arignac in my professional capacity. As I mentioned, I'm on vacation myself. Your godmother is an old and dear friend of mine, and my work there is very much a labour of love. So you're going to have to accept my presence, Marguerite—whether you like it or not.'

She moved restively. 'For how long?'

His meditative glance swept her, sending another quiver of uneasiness through her body. 'As long as it takes.'

'Meaning?' she asked thickly.

The dark eyes were enigmatic. 'She needs us both, Marguerite. That's all that matters. Now will you get in the car, or do you wish to stand here and argue until we get heatstroke?'

She complied reluctantly. So much for Haut
Arignac providing a sanctuary, she thought with
irony, as the car moved forward. Jerome Moncourt's web spread wide, it seemed.

And this could well turn out to be the longest
four weeks of her entire life.

They came to Haut Arignac just before noon. It
had been a journey filled with tensions. Not a great
deal had been said by either of them. Jerome had
politely drawn her attention to various landmarks
and points of interest along the way. She had re-
sponded largely in monosyllables, only permitting
herself to betray any real interest when they reached
the village of Arignac, from which the château de-
rived its name.

It was only a small community, held peacefully
in the curve of a meandering river. The houses were
built from rose-flushed stone, and a huge medieval
church like a small cathedral brooded over the main
square with its fringe of plane trees.

Jerome pointed to it. 'Built by the Crusaders in
thanksgiving for their victory over the Cathars,' he
told her. His mouth twisted. 'A slight over-reaction,
since they outnumbered them four to one.'

'From what I've read so far, it was a ghastly
campaign all round,' Meg said, shuddering.

Beyond the village, a faded fingerpost, half-buried in long grass at the side of the road, pointed them over an ancient stone bridge. There was always something about crossing a river, Meg thought. As if each one was some personal Rubicon, from which there was no turning back.

Which was exactly her own position, of course. Once she arrived at the château, she was committed to the part she'd agreed to play, however distasteful she found it. The die was cast, and she was Margot.

But Madame de Brissot would never know, or suffer by the deception, she told herself with determination.

And the man beside her would simply never know...

Beyond the bridge, the trees closed in like some green and sun-dappled tunnel. The road was climbing perceptibly, and ahead of her she could see tall wrought-iron gates, standing open between massive stone pillars, crowned with eagles.

Jerome turned the car through the gates on to a drive, which was broad but neglected, with moss and grass sprouting through the centre of its worn surface. The trees and bushes on either side needed cutting back, and the undergrowth was running riot.

As they rounded a long, curving bend, Jerome braked gently. 'The best view is from here,' he said.

He wasn't exaggerating, Meg realised, as she bent forward with a gasp of delight. The Château Haut Arignac was a gracious country house, built on a slight eminence in the middle of rolling parkland, like an island of stone in a sea of grass. It was an elegant rectangle of a house, built on three storeys, the severity of its lines tempered by a pepper-pot tower at each end, and by the broad raised terrace which surrounded it. The faded earthy pink of the roof tiles contrasted with the grey stone walls, and the tall windows on the two lower floors were masked by white shutters, like closed eyelids, as if the house drowsed in the midday sun.

Jerome parked below the terrace on a square patch of gravel. He motioned Meg to go ahead of him up the broad flight of shallow steps leading to the main entrance.

The air was hot and very still, and her heels seemed to echo as she crossed the stone flags. As she got nearer, she saw that Jerome's comment about the best view had been slightly ironic. The château's façade was altogether more elegant at a distance. Close to, it was apparent that the paint-work and pointing of the masonry needed renewing, and several of the ground-floor shutters needed repairing, and were hanging from their hinges.

In fact, it was all rather run-down. Maybe Margot's potential inheritance wasn't the gilt-edged security she'd imagined after all, Meg thought drily.

As she reached the heavy door, it swung open, and she found herself confronted by a small roly-poly woman in a dark dress, her eyes twinkling in welcome.

'Come in, *mademoiselle*. *Madame* told me to keep watch for you.' She looked past Meg, her smile widening to a beam. 'Monsieur Jerome.'

'*Ca va*, Philippine?' Jerome looked at Meg. 'Margot, this is Madame Lange, who keeps house here.'

She's got a job on her hands, Meg thought, her nose detecting a faint but pervading odour of damp. The hall itself was lofty, its painted ceiling rioting with rather grimy gods and goddesses. The walls were panelled in dark wood, and hung with pictures which seemed mainly to be portraits. The de Brissot ancestors, no doubt, Meg thought as she was led across to a pair of double doors.

Philippine threw them open with a flourish. 'Mademoiselle Margot is here at last, *madame*.'

Fighting back her trepidation, Meg walked into the room. She found herself in a large *salon* over-looking the gardens at the back of the house. The French windows leading to the terrace were ajar, but the shutters were half closed to exclude the fierceness of the sun, and Meg had to peer to discern her hostess.

Margaret de Brissot was sitting in a striped satin chair beside the empty marble fireplace, a slight upright figure in a navy silk dress, with snow-white hair arranged in a formal chignon. Her face was masked by a pair of tinted glasses, and a silver-topped cane rested against her chair.

She held out a commanding hand. 'Welcome to Haut Arignac, my dear child.' Her voice was clear and crisp, belying the fragility of her appearance. 'A little more light now, Philippine, if you please.'

The other woman opened the shutters, and sunlight flooded in, revealing, with less than kindness, the faded grandeur of the room. Meg's hand was taken with surprising firmness, and she was drawn down into a swift, formal embrace, *madame*'s papery cheek placed fleetingly against hers.

'It has been a long time, my dear. Too long, and for that I blame myself.' She sighed faintly. 'Your mother and I were never—close, and after your dear father's death I made little effort to maintain any real contact between us. Which I have come to regret, with the passage of time. My companion Sylvie's absence seemed to offer an opportunity to—heal the breach.'

'She never liked me.' Iris Langtry's pettish words echoed in Meg's mind. 'Never thought I was good enough for her beloved nephew.'

Meg said gently, 'I understand.'

Madame de Brissot's fingers tightened on hers. 'So shall we abandon the foolish pretence that we remember each other, and begin our acquaintance from this minute?'

Meg nodded. 'I—I'd like that, *madame*.'

The thin face relaxed into a smile. 'Then, perhaps for your father's sake, you would call me "Tante" as he did.'

This was where the guilt began, Meg thought bleakly. She forced a smile of her own. 'Of course. I'd like that.'

Madame de Brissot looked at Jerome. 'She's charming, isn't she, *mon cher*? And you are so good to have brought her to me.'

He took her hand and kissed it. 'It was my pleasure, believe me.' His eyes, hooded and expressionless, met Meg's, who found involuntary colour stealing into her face.

'I hope so.' *Madame* lowered her voice conspiratorially. 'I am relying on you, Jerome, to ensure that Margot is not bored during her stay here.' She turned to Meg. 'He was completely against my inviting you, my dear. And he has a point, of course. It is expecting a great deal—too much, perhaps—to ask a lively young woman to give up her busy life and spend a quiet month in the country, dancing attendance on a virtual stranger.'

Meg lifted her chin. 'Really? Is that Monsieur Moncourt's considered opinion? It isn't mine. I'm happy to be here with you—Tante.'

Madame took Meg's hand and patted it. 'You hear that, Jerome? All the same, we must try to make her stay an interesting one.'

Meg bit her lip. 'I don't require a great deal of entertainment,' she said with a touch of desperation. 'Being part of the family is quite enough. And I certainly don't want to be any further bother to Monsieur Moncourt,' she added with cold emphasis. 'I know he has his hands more than full already.'

And he could read whatever he wished into that, she told herself, watching his firm mouth twist with a kind of wry acknowledgement.

'But you will have a great deal of spare time to fill,' *madame* pointed out. 'My doctor insists—so foolish—that I rest, morning and afternoon.'

Meg said with finality, 'I'll be fine, I promise you.' She smiled at the older woman. 'All this is so new to me. I know I can find plenty to occupy me.'

'Searching for more traces of the Cathars, perhaps?' Jerome suggested softly. He turned to *ma-*

dame. 'Your new companion, *ma chère*, is studying the history of the Albigensian Crusade.'

'A sad and bloody period in the history of the Languedoc.' *Madame's* brows lifted. 'And a curious interest, too, for someone so young and lovely.' Her expression became faintly roguish. 'Now the troubadours—the Courts of Love—that I could understand.'

'Clearly Mademoiselle Margot has hidden—and unexpected—depths.' Jerome's tone was silky. 'I wonder what other surprises she has in store for us?' He paused. 'Apart, of course, from her excellent French.'

'*Vraiment?*' *Madame's* face was astonished. 'But your mother's letter, my dear, stated quite categorically that you couldn't speak a word of the language.'

Meg groaned inwardly. 'She didn't ask me, actually.' She tried to sound casual, even faintly amused. 'And my marks at school, admittedly, were never that good. All those irregular verbs.' She shrugged, pulling a laughing face. 'I guess she simply—took it for granted that nothing had changed.'

'A grave mistake. I am beginning to see that with you, *ma belle*, nothing should ever be taken for granted.' The dark face was sardonic. 'I think the month ahead of us is going to be fascinating—and most instructive.'

'You see,' *madame* exclaimed triumphantly, 'I made exactly the right choice, after all.' She turned to Meg. 'Now Philippine will show you to your room, my dear, and, when you have refreshed yourself a little, we can have lunch.'

Meg was thankful to escape from the *salon* without her legs buckling under her, or nervousness making her throw up on the faded Aubusson carpet.

Well, she'd had her baptism of fire, and survived, she thought shakily, as she followed Philippine's sturdy form up the gracious sweep of the stairs. But she didn't like herself any the better for it. The fact remained that she was an intruder in *madame*'s house, accepting her hospitality—and her affection—under totally false pretences.

That was quite bad enough. But Jerome Moncourt's presence made everything a hundred times worse. A nightmare from which there would be no reassuring awakening, she thought, her throat tightening with unease. His whole attitude to her was disturbing—a total enigma. Or was it merely sexual pique because she'd walked out on him?

For her own peace of mind, she would have to stay out of his way as much as possible, she told herself. That might not be easy. But at least she'd have the evenings to herself when he went back to the *mas*, and his own private life.

She found herself remembering the black and silver bed, and the panorama over the eastern hills, wondering how many women had watched the dawn, there in his arms. *'Ah God, ah God ...'*

The pain that went through her was like a knife, slashing and savage, resembling nothing she'd experienced before in its sudden intensity.

She thought, If I didn't know better, I'd almost think I was jealous. But it can't be that. It can't be ...

And this time the tremor that shook her was not of pain, but of fear.

CHAPTER SIX

'THIS is your room, *mademoiselle*.' Philippine's prosaic words rescued Meg, snatching her back from the whirling edge of some emotional abyss.

'Oh—thank you.' Her heart still thudding wildly, in revolt against that sudden moment of wholly unwelcome self-revelation, Meg went through the door that Philippine was holding open.

She found herself in a large square room, made gloomy by an assortment of heavily carved old-fashioned furniture and a big, canopied bed. The smell of damp was even more pronounced than it had been downstairs, but the bed seemed soft enough in spite of its faintly oppressive appearance, and the linen was crisp and fragrant with dried herbs of some kind, she realised appreciatively.

'I hope you will be comfortable.' Philippine fussed anxiously with towels. 'The bathroom is across the passage.' She pointed to its door. 'It is the only one in this part of the house, so you share it with Monsieur Moncourt.'

Meg swung round. 'But he doesn't stay here, surely?' She paused, trying to moderate the startled sharpness of her tone. 'I mean—he has a house of his own—not far away—doesn't he?'

'Ah, yes.' Philippine shrugged largely. 'Sometimes he returns there at night. Sometimes not.' She glanced around her. 'To survey a house of this size in a limited time, and prepare a list of works, is a task of great magnitude. Often *monsieur* begins early in the morning, and is occupied very late at night, so it is more convenient for him to stay.'

She gave Meg a darting smile. 'Besides, *madame* likes him to remain. She enjoys much to have the company of a man in the house once more, I think.' She sighed sentimentally. 'He is like the son she never had, *la pauvre*.'

'Really?' Meg kept her voice non-committal, but her heart sank like a stone.

'Now I must prepare to serve lunch.' Philippine took a last look round, and pointed to a frayed cord hanging beside the bed. 'If there is anything you require, *mademoiselle*, you must ring.'

'I'm sure everything's fine.' Meg forced a smile of her own. She'd just seen that the heavy door sported an ornate lock, complete with key. Rusty, maybe, but hopefully still functional. Just in case Monsieur Moncourt decided he wanted to share more than a bathroom, she told herself grimly.

When Philippine had bustled off, she went to have a look at the bathroom. There was a bolt on this door too, she saw with satisfaction.

The tub was a massive affair, standing on claw feet in the centre of the room, in a kind of majestic isolation. Meg's tentative manipulation of one of the heavy brass taps brought an instant gush of steaming water, and she patted the bath's substantial cast-iron side.

I think we may be friends, she told it under her breath. She wished she could sink into its depths right now, and soothe away her growing unease and uncertainty, but with lunch imminent the best she could hope for was a quick rinse of her face and hands in the large hand-basin.

She went back across the passage to collect a towel, and stopped dead in the doorway with a little gasp as Jerome Moncourt turned, hands on hips, from the window.

He looked, Meg thought angrily, quite unnervingly at home. 'What are you doing here?' she demanded between her teeth. 'You've got a hell of a nerve.'

'Don't be more of a fool than you can help,' Jerome retorted crisply. He pointed to the corner of the room. 'I've just carried up your luggage. It begins to be a habit.'

'Thank you,' Meg said stiffly. 'But I still want you out of here.' She crossed to the bed and grasped the bell-pull. 'Or do I have to ring for Madame Lange?'

'Summon whoever you wish,' he said pleasantly. 'But don't tug too hard or the whole mechanism will undoubtedly come away in your hand, and bring the whole ceiling with it. Philippine should have warned you.'

'I don't believe you.'

He laughed. 'It's a possibility. Word of an architect.'

Meg took a breath, relinquishing the rope with open reluctance. 'I don't think I'd take your word for what day it was,' she said with bitter clarity.

'Harsh words.' His voice was dry. He looked her over, the hooded eyes meditative. 'I think you and I must declare a truce.'

'On whose terms?' She faced him, chin up, eyes sparkling, refusing to admit to herself the potency of his attraction. 'And for how long? Oh, don't tell me.' She gave a small, brittle laugh. 'As long as it takes.'

'Exactly that. There is a great deal to be accomplished, as you've already noticed.' He looked around him. 'I hope you're not too disappointed in your surroundings,' he went on coolly. 'You'd imagined, perhaps, something more glamorous—

and definitely more affluent.' He shook his head. 'Without money to halt the decline, a house like this can become more of a burden than an asset.'

'That's hardly any concern of mine,' she said brusquely. 'And I don't think Madame de Brissot would care to have her private affairs discussed behind her back, no matter how old a friend you might be.'

'I stand corrected.' A faint smile twisted the corners of his mouth. 'So you've never wondered about the future, Marguerite—asked yourself what this frail elderly godmother of yours might have in mind for her crumbling heritage? Or why she has chosen to summon you here at precisely this moment in time?'

'No,' Meg said baldly. 'I haven't.' Yet wasn't this exactly why she was here—to safeguard Margot's mercenary interests? her conscience nudged at her. Although these seemed to be fading fast, she acknowledged in silent satisfaction.

Jerome laughed. 'You are almost too good to be true, *ma belle*.' There was a jeering note in his voice. 'I look forward to the—furtherance of our relationship over the weeks to come.'

'Well, I don't share your sense of anticipation.' Meg lifted her chin. 'And we don't have a relationship, as far as I'm concerned,' she added for good measure.

'No?' He studied her, brows lifted. 'My recollection is rather different.'

'Perhaps,' she said grittily. 'I remember—a temporary aberration. Nothing more.' She drew a breath. 'In fact, *monsieur*, I get the distinct impression that you don't even like me very much.'

'Liking?' His voice was contemptuous. 'What has that bland word to do with the flame of the senses between a man and a woman? Last night, Marguerite, your body cried out to mine. And nothing—no denials—no regrets—can change a thing.'

Two swift strides brought him to her. Before she could assimilate what was happening and take avoiding action, Meg found herself pulled into his arms, pinioned with merciless strength against the hard length of his body. His thigh thrust between hers, parting her legs in harsh and devastating intimacy. Her lost and frightened cry was stifled in her throat as his mouth closed hungrily on her trembling lips.

The kiss seemed endless—eternal. She couldn't breathe, and sparks of fire danced behind her closed eyelids. She could hear the thunder of her pulses, like the reverberations of yesterday's storm, feel the blood running thick and hot in her veins. Reason was suspended. In spite of herself she was transformed into sheer physical sensation.

Jerome's hands slid down her spine, cupping her buttocks, urging her towards him, to the fierce, compelling pressure of his muscular thigh against the moist, soft centre of her womanhood.

Oh, God, she screamed wordlessly, as her body ground eagerly, greedily against his, seeking an assuagement she could only imagine. Every fibre of her being was focused with an almost savage intensity on the burn of his mouth and body against hers, until she thought she was going to faint—or die.

The bed was so close. All she had to do was sink back on to it, pulling him down with her... And then, with devastating suddenness, she was free again. Jerome tore his lips from hers, putting her away from him almost roughly. His hooded eyes glittered, and there was a faint sheen of sweat on his forehead.

He said raggedly, 'So let's not talk of aberrations, my beautiful little hypocrite. Because now we both know better.' He paused, his eyes raking her flushed, aroused face. 'Don't we, *ma poule*?'

He turned, and strode to the door. Meg watched dazedly as he took the key from the lock, tossing it almost reflectively in his hand, as he glanced back at her. He said, half to himself, 'I think this will be safer with me,' and walked out of the room, leaving her there, bereft, one hand pressed to her bruised and quivering mouth.

It took all Meg's courage to go downstairs again. She was desperately tempted to cry off from lunch—to plead a headache, or some other excuse. But to do that would be tantamount to admitting he'd achieved some kind of victory, and that would be fatal.

She went into the bathroom, splashing cool water on her flushed face, then got to work with the modest supply of cosmetics she'd brought with her, trying to disguise with colour the swollen contours of her mouth, and shadow the almost drugged intensity of her eyes. But there was little she could do to control the unruly throb of her pulses, or the aching torment of need he'd awoken in her yet again.

In fact, he'd hardly had to try, she thought with a kind of icy despair commingled with shame. Now she had to face him—to pretend that nothing had happened. But then, on the face of it, very little had. He'd kissed her, that was all. A justification of his male ego, which she'd wounded. A mistake she would not make again, she thought flatly. She'd come here to be Madame de Brissot's companion, and only that. From now on she'd become her devoted shadow, never willingly prised from her side, she thought grimly.

And, in spite of his lethal attraction, there'd be little Jerome Moncourt could do about that. And, sooner or later, he'd get tired of his sterile pursuit of her, and devote himself to the lady on the telephone—or someone else on his list, leaving her free to go home at the end of the month, and forget him.

If she could.

Meg stared at her reflection, observing almost clinically the wide, troubled eyes, the tautness along her cheekbones, and the quiver of her bruised lips, felt the desolate pang of yearning vibrate deep within her, turning her whole body into a silent sigh of longing.

She thought with a kind of anguish, Oh, please God, don't let it be too late. Don't—don't let me be in love with him.

Head held high, she eventually descended the stairs, pausing at their foot to brace herself as she heard voices from the *salon*. Then quietly, she pushed open the door and walked into the room. *Madame* was occupying her former seat, a hand pressed rather wearily to her forehead, while Jerome was standing at the window, holding a sheaf of papers.

'If you think the work is necessary, then, of course, it must be done,' *madame* was saying as Meg entered.

He nodded, putting the papers into his briefcase. 'I will work out some figures and include them in my report,' he said. He frowned slightly. 'But I shan't be able to get it typed until Marie-Claude returns from her own leave, and the delay is a nuisance.'

'In that case, perhaps Margot could help you,' *madame* suggested suddenly. 'She works as a secretary to an English politician, I understand. She turned towards Meg. 'You would be happy to deputise for Marie-Claude, I'm sure, *ma chère*?'

Meg felt as if she'd been turned to stone. This was a snag neither she nor Margot had foreseen, she thought, a bubble of hysteria welling up inside her.

'Margot. You don't answer.' *Madame*'s tone held a hint of reproof, and Meg recovered herself.

She said coolly, 'I doubt if I can help. You see, I'm not really a typist—more of a personal assistant. Maybe my practical skills won't be up to Monsieur Moncourt's standard.'

For a moment, she seemed to encounter that strange, frozen anger again, then his smile slanted, and he shrugged. 'I will be happy to make use of whatever skills you have,' he said softly.

'Then that is settled,' Madame de Brissot approved. 'Now let us go into lunch.'

Leaning on her cane, she led the way into the dining-room. Meg followed, aware that her appetite had deserted her. The brief commercial course during her final year at school hadn't prepared her to be anyone's secretary, but that was almost immaterial compared with the personal implications facing her.

As she sat down, she gave Jerome a burning look across the table. There was mockery mingled with triumph and something else easily definable in his own gaze.

It was almost as if Madame de Brissot was trying to throw them together, she thought without pleasure as she drank her soup. She said, 'When do you want me to start work? This afternoon?'

'I am not such a slave-driver.' His smile slanted again, twisting her heart. 'Tomorrow is soon enough.'

Altogether too soon, Meg decided sombrely as Philippine cleared the plates, and brought in a platter of baked fish, supplemented by green beans and tiny new potatoes cooked in their skins and sprinkled with parsley.

'So tell us,' Jerome said when they were all served, and he had poured out pale golden wine from a carafe. 'What exactly are the duties of a personal assistant?'

Meg concentrated on removing a bone from her portion of fish. 'They vary,' she said at last.

'I'm sure they do,' he said silkily. 'But you must be able to name at least one.'

'Well—there's research.' She'd heard Margot mention that, she remembered with relief. 'And I help sort out problems in the constituency.'

'And you can abandon such responsibilities to spend four weeks here?' Jerome's brows lifted. 'If I were your boss, I wouldn't be pleased by such desertion.'

Meg stared at her plate. 'I have six weeks' leave a year,' she said quietly. 'How and when I take it is up to me. And it will soon be the summer recess anyway,' she added, hoping it was true.

'Nevertheless it is good of him to allow you to indulge me like this.' Madame de Brissot looked faintly troubled. 'I had not realised what problems it might cause when I issued the invitation.'

Jerome smiled at her. 'I don't think you need worry,' he said silkily. 'I'm sure our lovely Margot is a paragon among secretaries—far too valuable to lose.' His gaze meeting Meg's was like the clash of swords before some duel. She almost flinched under the impact. 'Isn't that so, *ma belle*?'

'That's not for me to say.' Her voice sounded wooden, even to herself.

He laughed softly. 'You're too modest.' He leaned forward suddenly. Like some predator, she thought with swift breathlessness, waiting to pounce. 'So tell us something about this prince among employers, Margot,' he prompted. 'What is he like?'

'I don't think any man is a prince in his secretary's eyes, *mon cher*,' *madame* put in with amusement. 'Usually she knows him too well—rather like a wife.'

'All the better.' Jerome's eyes were fixed on Meg's flushed downbent face, his own expression enigmatic. 'Such intimate knowledge should prove—most enlightening.'

Meg bit her lip. 'It's hardly ethical for me to discuss him,' she evaded.

'Oh, come,' Jerome urged mockingly. 'You are among friends, and nothing you say will go beyond these walls, so where is the harm?' He paused. 'I'm sure nothing damaging will emerge.'

Meg groaned under her breath. She wasn't going to be let off the hook, that was clear. They were both looking at her expectantly, and, in Jerome's case, with an odd intensity.

She ran the tip of her tongue round her dry lips as she thought rapidly about Steven Curtess. 'Well, he's dynamic and ambitious,' she began. 'A real go-getter and very hard-working,' she added rather lamely. It wasn't easy to paint a verbal picture of someone you'd seen on television and heard discussed in intimate detail all too often but never actually met, she thought with an inward grimace.

'Young or old?' Jerome queried.

Meg moved restively. 'In his thirties, I think.'

'You're not sure?' Jerome's glance was sceptical. 'Intimately acquainted as you claim to be with him?'

Meg lifted her chin at the faint sneer she thought she detected in his tone. 'I claimed nothing of the kind,' she denied coolly. 'That was your own idea, and not one I necessarily share.'

She saw Jerome's eyes narrow slightly. He paused. 'Even if you don't know his age, you'll be aware if he's married or single.'

'He's married.' Meg felt her flush deepen, as she wondered whether it was still true, or whether Margot's devious machinations had finally succeeded.

'And is he good-looking?' *madame* asked indulgently.

Meg shrugged again. 'I suppose—yes.' If you like that kind of thing, she added silently. Steven Curtess's rather florid brand of handsomeness had never had the slightest appeal for her.

Madame patted her hand. 'In your case, my dear, it sounds as if familiarity has indeed bred a soupçon of contempt,' she said with faint amusement. 'Well, perhaps that is not such a bad thing. Is he the only person you have worked for?'

'Yes.' Meg felt on safer ground here. Margot had gone straight from an expensive secretarial school to work for Steven Curtess in some private capacity in the City of London just before he'd decided to embark on a parliamentary career.

'So all your experience has been in one milieu.' Jerome sounded meditative. 'Then your boss may well be grateful to me for—broadening your horizons.'

Meg said shortly, 'Perhaps,' and prayed for a change of topic.

'I hope, that he is able to manage without you.' *Madame* signalled to Philippine to bring in the dessert of cheese and fresh fruit.

'No one's indispensable,' Meg said, ignoring Jerome's derisive smile.

'You're not afraid that when you return he'll have found someone else to take your place?' he asked softly.

Meg shrugged. 'That's a risk I'll just have to take.'

'Another?' His brows lifted. 'You like to live dangerously.'

She kept her smile bland, but her heart hammered as she thought, Not until now.

Within twenty-four hours her ill-advised masquerade could be over, and herself dismissed from Haut Arignac with all the ignominy she deserved. Because no one in his right mind was going to believe that the human dynamo she'd described would put up with her level of incompetence even for a moment.

I could bluff, she thought, but for how long? In a way, it would be a relief to be sent away, although her failure was going to cause all kinds of problems at home. But at least she would be removed from temptation where Jerome was concerned. If she was going to eat her heart out for him, it would be safer to do so at a distance.

'You are very quiet, *ma chère*,' *madame* observed. 'And you look sad—doesn't she, Jerome?'

'Perhaps she's homesick,' he said, as he peeled an apple. 'Pining for those she's left behind.'

'Of course. You must telephone your home, Margot. Reassure your mother that you are here and safe. You may use the phone in the library at any time. Jerome will show you where it is.' *Madame* reached for her cane. 'Now I am going to my room for this absurd rest.'

'Shall I come with you?' Meg asked awkwardly. She had no real idea what duties she'd be expected to perform.

'No, enjoy your freedom while you can. We have tea at four o'clock, and the English newspaper comes at that time. I like to have it read to me.' *Madame* shared a smile impartially between them. 'À bientôt, *mes amis*.'

Jerome opened the door for her, and she made her way slowly upstairs, attended by Philippine. Then he turned back to Meg. 'Now for the telephone.'

She hung back. 'There's no hurry, really.'

'One thing you should know at once is that your godmother's wishes are law in this house. She feels that your mother will be worried about you, and that her mind should be set at rest. That's all that matters.' His tone was brusque.

'Yes,' she said quietly. 'I—I didn't think.'

'Then have the grace to pretend. *Madame* is disposed to think well of you.' Jerome paused. 'I would not wish her to be disappointed—in any way.'

She lifted her chin. 'Nor would I—believe me.'

'Then perhaps we understand each other.' His faint smile was grim. 'Come with me, *ma belle*.'

As she followed him from the room, it occurred to her that she would go with him to the ends of the earth, if he asked. Which, she thought detachedly, must make me the biggest fool in creation.

And she wanted to weep for her own foolishness.

CHAPTER SEVEN

MEG put the receiver back on the rest with a faint sigh. She had tried to get through to her home three times, but each time the line had been engaged. She would have to try again later.

The de Brissot library certainly lived up to its name, she thought, glancing round her appreciatively. Apart from the space occupied by the inevitable French windows, the walls were lined, ceiling to floor, with books, many of them leatherbound and dating from other periods in the château's history.

She wandered over to the nearest shelf and began to glance along it, her excitement mounting as she examined the contents more closely. She dropped to her knees, pulling volumes out at random, her fingers reverent as she turned the pages.

One book seemed to have slipped down behind the others on the shelf. Meg saw that it was a collection of early French poetry, but a more modern edition than many of its companions.

She began to look through it, searching for the *aubade* Jerome had quoted to her, but to her disappointment it was not included in the selection, although most of the poetry, she realised, was about love. The language might be archaic but the message was familiar. Love sought, love fulfilled, and, even more potently, the loss of love—they were all there. As she read the lines, the grief and yearning that seemed to spring from the lines was as fresh and poignant as if the outrush of emotion which inspired it had been experienced yesterday, rather than the far-off days of the Middle Ages.

'You seem very absorbed,' Jerome's voice remarked behind her.

Meg started convulsively, dropping the book, as she swung round to face him. He was lounging in the doorway, hands in pockets, watching her.

She said huskily, 'You—you startled me.'

'Evidently.' His mouth twisted in faint amusement. 'Are you always so nervous?'

'Not usually,' she said tersely.

'So it's me,' he said softly. 'I'm amazed. I thought you were made of stronger stuff, *ma belle*.'

'But then,' she said, 'you know nothing about me.' She saw his smile widen, and flushed. 'I mean—nothing that really matters.'

'Perhaps we would differ on what those essentials are.'

'I think we'd probably differ on just about everything.' Meg retrieved her poetry book with hands that shook a little, and got up from the floor. 'Including my need for privacy. I'd like you to return the key to my bedroom door, if you please.'

'I am desolate to have to refuse you,' he said. 'But I think it is best that I keep it—as a safeguard, you understand. In your over-sensitive condition, *chérie*, you might be tempted to use it, and that would not be wise. The electrical wiring in this house is as decrepit as everything else, and if there was a fire you could be burned alive while we were breaking down your door.'

Meg met the mockery of his gaze, stony-faced. 'I can think of worse fates,' she retorted.

'I don't think so.' Jerome shook his head. 'Or has your reading about the destruction of the Cathars taught you so little?'

'Ugh.' She couldn't suppress the shudder that ran through her. 'I skipped a few pages after the surrender of Montségur.'

'No one could blame you for that.' He paused. 'What pages are you skipping now?'

'Very few.' She certainly wasn't going to tell him she was hunting for his *aubade*. She gestured around her. 'This is paradise. I wonder if *madame* realises how valuable some of these books are?'

His brows lifted mockingly. 'Calculating the assets, *ma belle*?'

She felt as if he'd slapped her across the face. She said bitingly, 'My interest is professional rather than personal, I assure you, *monsieur*.'

'You continue to astound me, my dear Margot,' he drawled. 'The Cathars—politics—and now rare books. Is there no limit to your expertise?'

'I'm no expert,' she muttered, her face flaming with guilty colour as she realised how nearly she'd given herself away. 'I had a—friend who dealt in antiquarian books. I helped out sometimes.'

'What a fascinating life you lead,' Jerome said softly. 'And what can I possibly offer to compensate you for the loss of it—temporarily, of course?'

He was still smiling, but there was an underlying hardness about his mouth, and his eyes were hooded again, their expression impossible to read. Meg was aware of a shiver of unease. She needed to get out of the room—to escape from this dangerous proximity. Only he was blocking the doorway—quite deliberately, she was certain.

'You don't need to offer anything,' she said steadily. 'I told you—I'm content in my own company. Besides this—month is for *madame*—for Tante.'

'What admirable devotion to duty.' His voice was harsh, flicking her like a whip. 'I hope you're a good actress, *ma belle*, because you'll need to be, I promise you.'

'Actress?' Meg felt swift colour flood guiltily into her face. 'What do you mean?'

Had that stupid slip over the books alerted him? she thought, desperately. Could he have guessed that she was an impostor? And, if so, what was he going to do about it?

His hand captured her chin without gentleness, turning her face up to his scrutiny. 'Such blushing innocence.' His tone was derisive. 'But we both know that's only a façade, don't we, *chérie*?' His voice quietened almost to a whisper. 'What are you doing here, Margot? What has lured you away from your work—your high-flying career—your many friends—to live in such rural seclusion for four long weeks?'

'*Madame* sent for me,' she defended.

'And you abandoned everything and everyone immediately.' He gave a soft laugh. 'One would almost think you were running away. From a situation you can no longer control, perhaps.'

'All that's running away is your imagination, *monsieur*.' Meg took a step backwards, freeing herself from his grasp. 'Nor do I see why I should have to submit to this kind of speculation,' she added with spirit. 'It's really none of your business.'

'You're wrong,' he said. 'Anything that affects Madame Marguerite is my concern, so be warned.'

Meg's laugh was almost brittle. 'Good heavens, *monsieur*.' She tried to copy Margot's insouciance. 'First your man Octavien gives me the hard word, and now you do the same. I'm beginning to regret that I ever came here. Now if you'll excuse me I need some fresh air.'

She headed for the French windows, praying they wouldn't be locked, but the handle turned easily in her grasp.

'I also have regrets.' Jerome's voice followed her harshly. 'I wish with all my heart, *ma belle*, that I had never met you. But it's too late now.'

Meg didn't look back, but his words seemed to re-echo in her head as she went into the sunshine. Too late, she thought. Far too late for her, when the wish of her own heart was centred irrevocably and eternally on Jerome Moncourt—who seemed only to despise her.

It was shatteringly hot. Not even the faintest breeze stirred the air as Meg went down the terrace steps to the garden. Even though she needed to be alone, perhaps this wasn't the best place to come in the heat of the day, she thought as she followed a ragged gravelled walk, searching for shade.

The garden had been allowed to decay in much the same way as the house, she realised sadly, pushing her way past overhanging shrubs and bushes. It would need a small army to restore it to order. She rounded a corner and stopped with a small sigh of pleasure as she saw where her path had led her. In a corner of the garden by a crumbling wall someone long ago had planted roses, some of the old, exquisite varieties she remembered from childhood. Rosa Alba, she thought, with a pang, Belle de Crécy, Ispahan, Rosa Mundi, and so many others. The roses her father had grown and loved in his own garden, nurturing them like delicate children.

Meg lifted her face, breathing in the warm scent with nostalgia. After her husband's death, Iris Langtry had rooted up all the old roses, and replaced them with scentless, disease-resistant hybrids. 'Far less trouble,' had been her brisk response to her stepdaughter's protests.

Meg sank down on the cracked stone bench. After years of being a widower, her father had met Iris and married her within a matter of weeks, showering her with passionate single-minded devotion that apparently saw no fault. He was lonely, she thought sadly, or else he might not have let himself fall for her so hard and so fast. And there was a lesson in that which she should take to heart in the current situation.

I'm lonely, too, she thought, and Jerome Moncourt is the first man to pay me any serious attention. But he's just amusing himself, and I must never forget that. Because I've seen how disastrous a whirlwind romance can be.

Admittedly, Iris had made her father happy for the last years of his life, and Meg could only be grateful for that. Her behaviour once she was his widow, with control over his estate, had been a different matter entirely, and Nanny's cottage was only one example of the way Iris had ignored or reinterpreted his known wishes.

Oh, Daddy, she thought sadly, why didn't you put it all in writing, instead of trusting her so completely? Because if you had I wouldn't be here today, on the edge of breaking my heart. I'd be safe...

The roses blurred suddenly into a mass of glittering colour, and she covered her face with her hands and wept the kind of shaking, scalding tears she hadn't allowed herself for years, the pain of loss commingling with her turmoil of emotion over Jerome.

'Marguerite.'

Because she'd been thinking about him, for a moment his voice seemed just another figment of her imagination. But the light touch on her shoulder was all too real, and she looked up with a gasp to see him, dark in the sunlight above her.

'What do you want?'

'*Madame* asked me to find you.' He studied her frowningly. 'What is wrong? Have you had bad news from home?'

She'd forgotten about her abortive phone call. She moved restively, dislodging his hand.

'It's nothing.'

'No one cries like this for nothing.' He took an immaculately folded handkerchief from his pocket and gave it to her, watching as she blotted the moisture from her face. The faint familiar musk of his cologne assailed her senses, and she fought back another sob, tautly aware of his regard.

He said softly, 'I don't think you have been wholly honest with me, *ma belle*.'

Her heart missed a beat. 'What do you mean?'

'You said there was no one in your life back in your own country. But that was a lie.' His voice hardened. 'Because those tears are for a man, aren't they? Answer me, Margot. Tell me the truth this time.'

Words of angry denial rose to her lips, but she suppressed them. If he thought she was in love with someone else, it would provide her with a shield to shelter behind—the excuse she desperately needed to hold him at arm's length.

She shook her hair back from her face defiantly, and looked at him. She said clearly, 'Yes—I'm crying because of a man. Someone I love. I admit it.' It was only the truth after all. If Jerome chose to interpret it in his own way, that was his business. 'Are you satisfied now?' Her tone was a challenge.

'Because I have made you confirm what I already knew?' His mouth twisted. 'There is, I suppose, a certain satisfaction in that.'

'So now will you leave me alone?'

He shook his head. 'That is impossible,' he said. 'And we both know it.' He picked up the book of poetry which had fallen to the grass beside her, and handed it to her. '*Madame* suggests, by the way, that we should go to Albi tomorrow to settle the business over the car.'

Meg said tautly, 'Thank you, but I can make my own way. I don't need an escort.'

His brows lifted. 'How do you propose to get there?'

'I suppose there's public transport?'

'There is a bus,' he agreed. 'But not tomorrow.'

Meg bit her lip. 'Then I'll use *madame*'s own car. Acting as her chauffeur was one of the reasons for coming here.'

'Yes, it was,' he said evenly. 'But I wish to assure myself that you are capable of handling her car safely.'

'How dare you?' Meg got to her feet. 'You know I can drive. I was driving when we met.'

'No,' he said. 'You were sitting in a stationary car, *ma belle*, waiting for a tree to fall on you. Not the same thing at all. So tomorrow your godmother wishes me to accompany you—to ensure that all is well. And now she is waiting for you. Unless you wish to continue this pointless argument, you are free to go.' As she went from him, Meg heard his voice add softly, 'This time.'

The shutters had been partly drawn in Madame de Brissot's room, and Meg was glad of the extra protection the ensuing dimness afforded. *Madame* was lying on the bed, propped up by pillows, her legs covered by a silk shawl. Her dark glasses had been discarded, and her face looked tired.

She greeted Meg with a faint smile. 'Come and sit by me, *petite*.' She held out her hand, closing it firmly round Meg's fingers. 'It is good to have you here. To give us both this chance to become friends. Do you agree?'

'Yes—yes, of course.' Meg felt like Judas.

'That makes me happy.' She was silent for a moment. 'Jerome, of course, had doubts. Your lifestyle in England—the gap in our ages. He felt I should have consulted him before inviting you.'

'Monsieur Moncourt,' Meg said steadily, 'seems to have things very much his own way here.'

'His family and ours were always neighbours,' Tante said, after another pause. 'I was—very glad when he returned to live at the *mas*. It has been too long without a master. And, of course, his arrival was a godsend to me because it meant I could make real plans, using his expertise, to renovate this house—to make good the neglect of past years.' She smiled. 'It has almost rejuvenated me too.' The clouded eyes peered at Meg. 'You are wondering, perhaps, why things have been allowed to slip so far—why there has been no proper maintenance?'

'It has occurred to me,' Meg admitted.

'It was not my wish,' Tante said slowly. 'But my husband would allow little or no money to be spent on the upkeep of the house. When he realised we would have no children—that he would be the last of his line—he seemed to lose all concern for the place. It was as if he wished it to crumble away. There was nothing I could say or do to persuade him otherwise.'

'That's a shame,' Meg said warmly. 'How could he bear to treat it like that?'

Tante gave a slight shrug. 'I think, like Madame de Pompadour it was a case of, "*Après nous le dé-*

luge,"' she said drily. 'Henri's interests lay else-where.'

'But it's such a beautiful place—or it could be.'

'It will be.' Tante spoke forcefully. 'Jerome is an expert at restoration. He will make Haut Arignac bloom again. You'll see.'

'I hope so,' Meg said with reserve.

'You don't sound too sure, *ma chère*.' Tante's lips curved. 'Yet you must trust him. I want you to be friends. It is important to me.' There was sudden urgency in her tone.

Meg said quietly, 'I—really don't know whether that's possible.'

'Oh, dear, is it that bad?' Tante's fingers tightened on hers. 'Your footsteps as you came along the corridor sounded flustered, I thought, and your hand is shaking a little. Has Jerome been torment-ing you, *le méchant*?'

Meg bit her lip. 'You—could say that.' Although she'd removed the worst of the tear-stains, she was glad *madame* couldn't see her face.

Madame de Brissot laughed. 'Oh, *la*.' There was a wealth of fondness in her tone. 'He is incorrigi-ble, that one. He loves to tease. So like his grand-father in so many ways, as well as being his namesake,' she added with a swift sigh. 'But, of course, he means no harm. You must believe that.

And after all to meet like that—thrown together by a storm—is almost romantic, don't you think?'

Meg bent her head. 'I was really too terrified to notice,' she returned.

'But you weren't harmed, thank God. And certainly thanks to Jerome.' *Madame* relinquished her hand gently. 'The Chinese,' she remarked, almost inconsequentially, 'believe that if you save someone's life you are responsible for that life forever after.'

'God forbid,' Meg forced a smile. 'I can take care of myself. And that's what you should be doing,' she added. 'I thought this was your rest period.'

'It's not easy for me to relax today.' Tante pulled a little face. 'To have you here with me—and my dear Jerome—under this roof. Such happiness.' She gave a little sigh. 'My mind is everywhere.'

'Would you like me to read to you?' Meg volunteered. 'The paper hasn't come yet, but I found the most wonderful book of poetry in the library.'

'You did?' Tante sounded almost startled. 'May I have it?'

Meg put the book in her hands, and watched as the thin fingers touched the covers and binding very gently.

She said, 'There is a poem that begins "*Ma doulce amour, ma plaisance chérie.*' Can you find that, my dear?'

She lay back, closing her eyes, as Meg began to read, a little awkwardly at first, her tongue stumbling over some of the archaic words and phrases. As she finished one poem, she went on to the next, letting her voice sink lower and lower, until Marguerite de Brissot's gentle breathing announced that she was asleep.

Meg let the book drop into her lap, and sat for a moment studying the patrician face now in repose. *Madame*'s bone-structure had defied time, she thought. There was no doubt that once she'd been very beautiful. She saw too the trace of a solitary tear on her cheek.

She glanced down at the book, wondering if it was the mention of her late husband, and the reminder of her own loss, which had caused the reaction. Maybe the book had belonged to him. Vaguely intrigued, she glanced at the flyleaf. There was an inscription, faded, but still legible.

'To Marguerite,' it said simply. 'My whole heart. J.'

Meg stared down at the initial. 'J', she thought. But Monsieur de Brissot's name had been Henri.

She closed the book with the uneasy feeling that she'd intruded into some very private domain. The book indeed had a special meaning for Tante still, but certainly not in the way she'd imagined, she thought wrily. Judging by what the older woman had told her, she seemed to have been left to her own devices a great deal. Had Henri de Brissot neglected his English wife in the same way as he'd disregarded his house?

His English wife...

'*Anglaise*' Octavien's voice, harsh with dismissal—with rejection—came back to her suddenly. Octavien who'd worked for the other—the first—Jerome Moncourt until he'd left the *mas* never to return.

She swallowed, as she remembered some of the words of passion and loss she'd just read aloud. Was that what had happened? she asked herself in astonishment. Had Jerome's grandfather fallen in love with his neighbour's beautiful lonely wife, only to renounce her at some point, and cut himself off forever from all his old ties? She wasn't sure what the implications of such an entanglement would have been, but there'd have been no easy divorce, that was certain.

Was this why the first Jerome de Moncourt had been forced to make a new life for himself in the city? And was this the reason for Octavien's bitter resentment of all things English—that the master he loved had been driven away because of his involvement with an *Anglaise*?

It all made a lot of ghastly sense, she told herself broodingly. And it explained Madame de Brissot's trust and affection for the present-day Jerome.

'Like the son she never had'. Philippine's words came back to her. Her heart missed a beat. And she, of course, was the almost forgotten goddaughter. Or so *madame* supposed, at least. A girl summoned out of the blue to this particular place, at this particular time. But for what reason?

'I want you to be friends. It is important to me'.

Meg swallowed. Perhaps she was being over-imaginative, but could there be a deeper purpose behind *madame*'s invitation than even Margot had figured out?

The son she'd never had, and the girl she'd lost touch with brought together under one roof—as Tante had just exulted. Thrown deliberately into each other's company for four long weeks under the hot sun of Languedoc. Was this *madame*'s secret plan—a romantic dream to re-create the past, and ensure that the heritage of Haut Arignac continued into another generation?

If so, it was total madness—doomed to failure for any number of reasons, the primary one, of course, being Meg's already deeply regretted imposture. And another was the 'old friend' who'd phoned him at the *mas*. There'd been no mistaking

the warmth in his voice. There was clearly a deep
bond of affection tying him to this other woman.

But how much did Jerome himself know of
Tante's scheme—if indeed it existed outside her
imagination? And, if he knew, was he really prepared to accept an arranged marriage to a stranger
in order to become master of Haut Arignac?
Having first cold-bloodedly swept her off her feet
into love with him, she reminded herself shakily.

Yet what did she really know about him? From
the very beginning, he'd been an enigma—a dark
figure conjured up out of the storm, and with the
same destructive elemental power.

She'd always expected that love, if and when it
came to her, would be a gentle thing, born from
friendship, nurtured by shared interests—not this
sweeping, headlong torment of heartache and desire, which he, God help her, didn't even share.
That was the bitter truth she had to hang on to, at
all costs, regardless of any other considerations.

His kisses—his caresses—had not been for her at
all, but 'Margot Trant'. And while she remembered that she could keep herself safe.

Quietly, she put the book back down on the table beside the bed, and tiptoed from the room.

CHAPTER EIGHT

MEG finished her coffee and polished off the last few crumbs of the *citron*-flavoured biscuit served with it. It had been pleasant to sit here in the shade of the awning provided by the street café, and watch the world go by, but now it was time to move on, and meet Jerome, as arranged, outside the south door of the cathedral.

She stifled a sigh, feeling a flutter of nervous excitement deep inside her. There had been no way to avoid his company today. She had put in a bid for independence at dinner the previous night, but Madame de Brissot had been adamant that he should accompany her to Albi—'For this first occasion, my dear.'

And Jerome had enjoyed her discomfiture. Immediately after dinner, he had bidden them goodnight, and departed, and Meg had carefully not allowed herself to speculate where he might be, or in whose company, during the oddly quiet evening which followed.

She had still been seething as she took the road from Arignac earlier that morning, operating the elderly but beautifully kept Citroën with punctilious correctness.

Eventually, Jerome had said with dangerous politeness, 'If you wish to reach Albi today, *ma belle*, I suggest you stop behaving as if I were your *moniteur*—and drive.'

The transaction over the hire car had been quickly and amiably completed, with Meg even being congratulated on her fortunate escape.

What escape? she thought grimly. Out of the frying-pan, into a roaring fire.

During the course of a restless night, she'd debated whether her best plan might not be to bring the whole charade out into the open, before more harm was done.

But the thought of the inevitable repercussions deterred her. She had to keep silent for Nanny's sake—and also for Madame de Brissot's, because Tante would be deeply offended to discover that her own god-daughter had actually blackmailed someone else into keeping her company, and hurt too. And there was enough sadness in her face already.

She wouldn't want to learn either that the real Margot was a mercenary self-seeking little bitch, in love with a married man, and that was the reason for the imposture. Much better to let Tante keep her illusions, as far as possible, she thought. Except where her own future with Jerome was concerned. Those plans would have to be knocked on the head without delay. Unless she was just imagining it all—leaping to absurd conclusions.

But somehow I don't think so, she told herself restively. She glanced at her watch, and signalled for the bill. Before she set off for their rendezvous at the cathedral, she had a phone call to make from the booth in the café. Tante had asked her the previous evening with a hint of reproach whether she'd managed to contact her home yet. She'd been directed to the phone in the *salon*, tensely aware that Tante could hear every word of a potentially awkward conversation, but to her relief the line had been engaged yet again.

As it was once more this morning, she found. How odd, she thought. Iris disliked the phone, and was anyway too cost-conscious to make prolonged use of it. She dialled again, this time to Nanny's number, and here there was no reply, either.

Well, she'd tried, Meg thought with a mental shrug, as she hung up. She'd have to make another attempt at the château, while Tante was resting, maybe.

Probably because of its stormy past, the cathedral had more the look of an armed fortress than a house of prayer. Jerome was already waiting for her under the ornate white stone porch on the south side of the building.

'Am I late?' Meg asked with a touch of constraint as she joined him.

'Admirably punctual.' He glanced at the huge red-brick building behind them. 'Do you wish to see the famous fresco of the Last Judgement, or would you prefer Toulouse-Lautrec?'

Meg was taken aback. 'I thought we'd be going straight back to the château.'

'Why?' His brows lifted. 'This is a beautiful city.'

'I'm sure it is,' Meg said stiltedly. 'But this isn't how—either of us would choose to spend the day.'

He was silent for a moment. 'Shall we declare another truce, Marguerite? While I show you the city?'

He had not, she thought, denied what she'd said. She looked at him uncertainly—saw the dark eyes alive and dancing, the smile that twisted his mouth, and felt the excitement inside her uncurl into recklessness.

She said, '*Soit*. So be it. But I'd rather skip the Last Judgement.'

'You don't think your sins would bear inspection?' There was a faint edge to his voice.

She said lightly, 'Perhaps I'm more of a Cathar— one of the Perfect Ones.'

She saw his mouth compress in slight wryness. He said, 'Then I'll take you to see another kind of perfection.'

The Toulouse-Lautrec collection was housed in the Palais de la Berbie, the old bishops' palace.

'It's almost like meeting old friends,' Meg said as she gazed at the famous Moulin Rouge posters of Jane Avril and La Gouloue.

'You like them?' he asked.

She nodded. 'Yes, maybe because they're so familiar. But if I'm honest I prefer those we saw earlier—the ones of his family and friends. They're so much—quieter—and more affectionate, somehow.' She sighed. 'I wonder what his life would have been like if he hadn't been crippled by brittle bones?'

'He would probably have led a more conventional existence—married—looked after his estates. Some of the passion and intensity of his work might have been diluted by domesticity.'

'It would be good to think of him being happy,' Meg said, rather wistfully.

'But happy endings are not always possible. Haven't you learned that yet?'

No, she thought, as they emerged once more into the sunshine. But I'm getting there.

He took her to the old part of the town, and she explored it with open delight, as they traversed the narrow streets with their overhanging timbered houses. The buildings which spilled down to the edge of the river were all of rose-red stone, including the great cathedral.

'The city, of course, gave its name to the Albigensian crusade against the Cathars,' Jerome told her. 'And traces of Catharism lingered on here even after the massacre at Montségur.'

'Yet there's no sadness here,' she said thoughtfully. 'Albi seems to be a place that's come to terms with its past.'

'Everything passes, in time,' he said.

Yes, she thought. And, given time, this senseless—destructive—infatuation will be forgotten too. It has to be.

'And now lunch,' he went on briskly.

'Have we got time for that?' Meg bit her lip. 'Shouldn't we be getting back?'

'At this time of day?' Jerome parodied horror. 'You must learn to think like a Frenchwoman, *ma belle.*'

His hand was under her arm as he guided her through the groups of tourists lingering on the pavement, sending an unwanted tingle of awareness through her body.

She said steadily, 'I don't think that's necessary—for the short time I'll be in France.'

'But perhaps,' he said, 'we can persuade you to stay longer.'

She shook her head, not looking at him. 'I don't think so.'

'You say that now, but who knows what the fates have in store for any of us?'

Meg decided to ignore that, and hung back. 'Anyway, I'm really not hungry.'

'Well, I am,' he said promptly. 'You can sit and watch me.' His hand took hers, pulling her along gently but firmly, giving her no choice but to go with him.

He took her to a small restaurant in a narrow side-street, already steadily filling up with customers. Meg found herself installed on a banquette with Jerome beside her, his lean thigh altogether too close to her own for comfort, as they scanned the various choices on the hand-written *carte*.

Meg had seriously intended to stay aloof from the proceedings, but the aromas drifting through from the kitchen became increasingly irresistible. Under Jerome's guidance, she found herself confronted by a dish of tiny, delicate ravioli made with anchovies, followed by a platter of succulent lamb, pink in the middle and flavoured with garlic and rosemary.

'I seem to do nothing but eat,' she said faintly, as eventually she put down her knife and fork.

'You could do with some extra weight,' he said, the dark eyes smiling at her under their heavy fringe of lashes. 'Not too much, of course.'

She felt herself flush, and to cover her confusion drank some of the rosé wine, served with their meal in a little jug.

'How easily you blush,' Jerome remarked. 'I had not expected that.'

Perhaps the wine had given her Dutch courage, because she said, 'What did you expect?'

He was silent for a moment. 'How can I say? It's certainly true that some of *madame's* recollections of you had caused me—concern. I did not wish her to hope for too much from this reunion.'

'You thought she'd be disappointed?'

Jerome shrugged. 'It was a possibility. After all, she had last seen you as a young child, and her impressions then had been—mixed.'

'Oh, dear.' Meg kept her tone light. 'Did I do something frightful?'

He shrugged. 'She remembered that you were spoiled—precocious—seeking to be the centre of attention, demanding your own way at all times.'

'In other words, a complete brat,' Meg said wrily. 'But I suppose it's a phase all children go through.' And some of them don't change, she thought, recalling Margot's ruthless self-will. 'Surely you don't condemn me for that?' She lifted her chin, her eyes searching his face. 'Or was there something else?'

His expression told her nothing. 'But what else could there be?' he said, after a pause. 'My sole wish is to protect Madame Marguerite. She has had enough unhappiness in her life.'

Meg stared down at the immaculate white tablecloth. 'Did you know her husband?'

He shook his head. 'Only by reputation. He has been dead for many years.' His tone seemed to signify that the passing of the late Henri de Brissot had been no great loss.

'I gather it wasn't a very successful marriage,' Meg said carefully.

'It was a disaster,' he said grimly. 'A brief infatuation which flared up and died within a year, leaving them tied to each other. Henri disliked living in the country, so he left Marguerite alone at the château to manage his inheritance, while he spent his life at racecourses and casinos. He returned only when he was short of money. Sometimes there would be brief reconciliations, then he would become bored and restless again, and leave.'

'Did she tell you all this?' Meg asked with faint surprise.

Jerome hesitated. 'No,' he said shortly. 'Not all of it.'

Meg drank some of her coffee. Her conclusions hadn't been so far-fetched after all, she thought soberly. Where else could Jerome have learned the sad details of Tante's marriage but from his grandfather?

She said, 'Tante explained to me why the château was in such disrepair. It's—good that she's decided to do something about it.'

'Excellent.' His tone was dry.

'I wonder why she's waited until now?'

Jerome shrugged again. 'I suggest you ask her.' His tone was not encouraging.

Her fingertip traced the pattern on her saucer. She said a little breathlessly, 'I—get the idea that Tante's trying to—re-create the past in the present to some extent.' She swallowed. 'Do you know—do you understand what I'm talking about?'

'I think so.' The dark face gave nothing away, so she ploughed on.

'I thought you would.' Her mouth felt suddenly dry. 'I—must tell you that what Tante wants is—totally impossible. It can never happen.' She swallowed. 'I thought I'd better make that clear.'

'There's no need.' Jerome summoned the waiter with the bill.

'I think there is. The whole idea is—was—quite absurd.'

His smile was brief and impersonal. 'Completely ridiculous, *ma belle*. Don't trouble yourself about it any more.'

She said, 'But I had to mention it—because if I have to—work for you—we'll be obliged to spend a lot of time together.'

'As you say.' Jerome counted out notes from his wallet, and added a tip. 'Starting this afternoon,' he added silkily.

Meg's heart sank like a stone, but she rallied. 'So, I want to establish a—a totally professional relationship from now on.'

'As you have with your employer?'

She bit her lip again. 'Of—course.'

'*Vraiment*? You tell me, that in all the time you have worked for this man—this young, good-looking, high-powered man—you have not asked yourself what he would be like as a lover? That he has not seen the way your body moves under the so-demure clothes, or tried to awaken the sleeping fire in you?'

'Believe what you want,' Meg said shakily. 'What I'm trying to say is that I don't—I'm not prepared to be harassed in any way while I'm working for you, and if you won't agree, then the deal's off. And I shall tell Tante why.'

His mouth twisted. 'You think she would be outraged? I wonder. In view of her—foolish dreams about the pair of us, perhaps it would please her to know that I wanted to make love to you.' The dark eyes held hers. 'The past re-creating the present—isn't that your apt phrase?'

She said crisply, 'But she might not appreciate the fact that you were simply amusing yourself—especially if I told her we both had—other commitments.'

He was silent for a moment, the firm mouth hardening. But he didn't deny what she'd said. 'And you *ma belle*,' he said at last. 'Are you so sure that you'll be able to maintain this—professional distance during the hours we'll be alone together?'

'Yes.' She could feel the thud of her heart against her ribcage. She thought achingly, I've no choice. Oh, God, I've got to. . .

He laughed. 'How certain you are.' His eyes swept her mockingly. 'Yet I guarantee, *ma douce*, that you will be the first to break this—restraint you have imposed.' His voice sank almost to a whisper. 'You will come to me, Margot, because you cannot help yourself. You know it, and so do I.'

He'd got to his feet. Meg rose too, facing him. She said huskily, 'I accept your challenge, *monsieur*. And I warn you, I shall fight—every inch of the way.'

'So the truce is over.' His voice was soft. 'So be it.' He took her hand and lifted it to his mouth. She felt, with a jolt, his teeth graze her soft fingertips in a swift, sensuous caress.

He said, 'Now let us go back to Haut Arignac, and test your resolve.'

And led the way back to his car.

She sat beside him, prey to a total confusion of thought and conflict of emotion, out of which only one thing seemed clear—that her relationship with Jerome was not merely a question of self-control, but self-preservation.

Obsessed as she was with her predicament, she didn't notice at first that they'd turned off the Arignac road.

It was only when they reached the track leading down to the *mas* that comprehension dawned, and she sat up sharply.

'Where are we going?'

'To fetch my typewriter. There isn't one at the château. Madame Marguerite still prefers her correspondence to be hand-written.'

It sounded a reasonable explanation, but Meg stiffened.

'Do we have to begin today? Can't you bring it over in the morning?'

He sent her a brief, mocking smile. 'Tonight I shall be staying at the château. I have a room there. I'm sure Philippine has mentioned it.' He paused.

'Besides, the sooner our professional relationship begins, the better. I'm sure you agree, *ma belle*.'

He brought the car to a halt in front of the *mas*, and opened his door. 'Would you prefer to wait for me here?' There was amusement in his voice.

She said curtly, 'Fine.'

As he reached to door of the *mas*, Octavien emerged, and they stood talking for a moment. It had to be some urgent topic, because Octavien was gesticulating forcefully, his wrinkled face frowning with concern. And after a moment she saw Jerome swing round and send a swift, equally grim look back at the car.

She thought, They're talking about me. And a groundswell of resentment rose inside her. She opened the passenger door and got out, making a wide and pointed detour away from them, around the side of the house, where the terraces of vines clothed the side of the valley, and stood, staring out over the neat rows, listening to the whirr of the unseen cicadas in the undergrowth.

She heard a stone rattle on the track behind her, and turned to see Octavien coming towards her, a hoe on his shoulder. His face was set grimly, the dark eyes suspicious and openly hostile under the jutting brows. His reply to her quiet, '*Bonjour*,' was a curt nod.

She said, 'Maître Octavien, it was your *patron's* idea to bring me here today, not mine. But you need not worry.' She lifted her chin. 'I—I know what you fear, and I want to tell you that—it won't be like before. Not as it was with Monsieur Jerome's grandfather.'

She paused, but he said nothing, his expression not encouraging. She went on with a touch of desperation, 'I won't be coming back here—to the *mas*—again. And at the end of the month I'll be returning to England anyway, for good.' She tried a small, wintry smile. 'This Monsieur Jerome won't be driven away from here—at least, not by me.'

There was no softening in his face. He said in his hoarse *patois*, 'Whether he goes or stays, you bring unhappiness with you, *Anglaise*. I know that, me. I hear, and I see.' He nodded. 'You have no business here, and Monsieur Jerome should not concern himself with you—or the suffering you have caused.' His fist clenched, punching the empty air. 'Always unhappiness,' he muttered. He gave her a last fulminating look, then went on to the vines.

Well, I tried, Meg consoled herself, as she turned away. She looked up at the *mas*, at the big picture window on the upper floor, from which she would never now see the dawn, and stopped dead.

There was someone there, she thought. Someone looking down, and then moving away quickly as if they didn't want to be seen. She'd only caught the briefest glimpse, but she knew it was a woman. And not Berthe.

Her heart was thudding, leaden against her ribs. Well, what did she expect, after all? As she'd said herself, they both had—other commitments. But to say it was one thing. To face up to it in reality quite another.

When she reached the car, Jerome was closing the boot, his face set and preoccupied. And who can wonder? Meg asked herself bitterly. She wanted to say, Weren't you expecting company? And did she give you a hard time, when she saw you drive up with me? But pride kept her silent. Better for him not to know she'd seen his guest at all, let alone that she cared she was there. That would be altogether too much of a betrayal.

No wonder Octavien was so unwelcoming, she thought, her throat tightening. Presumably he approves of the lady waiting in the bedroom, and doesn't want anything—or anyone—to make waves. Least of all me.

Well, he doesn't have to worry. Because I know now, beyond all doubt, that I have nothing to hope for from Jerome. That I never did.

And she felt more desolate and alone than she'd ever been in her life before.

CHAPTER NINE

THE atmosphere in the car was loaded—charged with tension.

Jerome, lost in thought, made no attempt to initiate any immediate conversation, and Meg was thankful for it. It gave her time to pull herself together, recover at least the appearance of composure.

How quickly things could change, she thought shakily. Only an hour or so before they'd been companions, almost friends. Now the truce was over, and the swords were out again.

She stole a glance at him. There was tautness in every line of his face. If he was thinking about the woman at the *mas*, his train of thought didn't seem to be providing him with any particular pleasure. She could sense that hidden anger in him, like some volcano waiting to erupt.

Perhaps her appearance at the *mas* had caused some serious breach between them which couldn't be simply shrugged off. But that was hardly her fault.

'What were you saying to Octavien?' His voice broke abruptly across her troubled reverie.

'A touch of reassurance, which didn't work.' She paused, adding carefully, 'Octavien doesn't want any re-creation of the past either.'

Jerome too was silent for a moment. Then he said, 'You must forgive him. He was totally devoted to my grandfather from the time they roamed these hills together as boys. He saw only a future of companionship and hard work, bringing the *mas* back to life, extending the vineyard—seeing their children grow up together in turn.' He sighed sharply. 'Disappointment has made him bitter.'

Meg said slowly, 'And he blames Tante for—all of it. That isn't fair.'

'Why do you say that?'

'She was married. Your grandfather was a single man. Maybe he should have held back—thought twice before becoming involved. He had less to lose.'

'An interesting viewpoint,' he said softly. 'Yet the marriage was over before his intervention. He was not breaking up a relationship. Now that— *that*, *ma belle*, would be truly unforgivable. Don't you think?'

She said quietly, 'Perhaps none of us is qualified to pass judgement—at this distance.'

'Well, Octavien thinks otherwise. He feels that your godmother should have remembered her marriage vows, even if her husband did not.' He shook his head. 'Perhaps some of the old Cathar morality still lingers in the earth and stones of the Languedoc.'

Meg was silent for a moment. She said, 'But once she'd—broken her vows, why didn't she leave—walk out on the marriage once and for all? She could have made a whole new life with your grandfather. There was no need to make them both miserable.'

'It was not so simple. Perhaps it never is.' His voice was heavy. 'Henri de Brissot made it clear he would never willingly let her go, and that divorce was out of the question. Family pride was at stake, and he was prepared to use all the power of Church and State to force Marguerite to stay in the marriage.

'She had discovered, you see, that she was pregnant.' His mouth curled. 'And Henri had decided the child was his.'

Meg stared ahead of her. 'Was that—possible?'

Jerome lifted a shoulder. 'He still insisted on his conjugal rights,' he said flatly.

'How could she bear it?'

'She had little choice in the matter. And each time Henri reappeared he was full of repentance—

determined to put their relationship on a new footing, and make it work. She felt it was her duty to stay with him—and try again. Grandfather could not persuade her to change her mind. He was prepared to risk anything—any scandal—to have her with him. But her prime consideration was—had to be—the child.

'Because Henri could just have been right. That was what haunted her—what swayed the balance in the end.'

Meg touched the tip of her tongue to her dry lips. 'But—there was no child.'

'As it turned out, no. There was an accident—the ultimate irony. She slipped on the stairs one day, when she was alone in the house. It almost cost her her life as well as the baby's.' He was quiet for a moment. 'Henri, of course, never forgave her. That was the end of any hope for the marriage. She had sacrificed herself and her happiness in vain.'

'But what about your grandfather?'

'He swore if he left it would be forever, and he meant it, although he didn't blame Marguerite for the choice she'd made.'

He paused again. 'So he went to Paris first, then abroad, to manage a property in Martinique that had belonged to his mother's side of the family. While he was on leave, he met my grandmother, and made a new life for himself.'

'Were they happy?'

'They were certainly profoundly content. Perhaps that is a safer basis for a relationship that must last a lifetime.'

Perhaps, Meg thought, with a catch in her throat. But it sounded very much like second best to her— a thought which occupied her in silence until they reached Haut Arignac.

Jerome, she learned, had decided to establish his temporary office in the library.

She looked round her. Suddenly the dark, book-lined walls seemed hostile, as if they were closing in on her, holding her prisoner. As maybe they were. She looked with loathing at the sleek electronic typewriter with the built-in screen, which he'd brought in from the car and placed in the centre of the big table.

And that, of course, was to be her instrument of torture in this dungeon, she thought, her lips twisting.

'I've never used this particular model before,' she said, watching Jerome plug it into the power supply. Or anything remotely like it, she added silently. The typewriter at the bookshop, which she'd used occasionally for correspondence and invoices, had been a portable, manual machine of roughly the same vintage as many of the books, but at least she'd felt in control.

Whereas this thing had a memory, and presumably also a mind of its own...

'It has all the standard features. There should be no problem.' He stood up, dusting his hands, then took a folder from his briefcase. There were pages of notes inside, in his crisp, incisive handwriting. Reams of the stuff, Meg thought glumly.

'If you could make three copies?' He glanced at his watch. 'I'll come back in an hour to see how you're getting on.'

Well, at least that was better than having him standing over her, watching her fumble her way to disaster, Meg decided as the door closed behind him. Wasn't there a fairy-story about a girl who'd been locked into a tower, and ordered to spin straw into gold, on pain of some ghastly fate?

I know how she felt, Meg told herself, as she assembled paper and carbons. But no magical power was going to perform any miracles to save her, she soon realised, as the waste basket began to fill up with spoiled sheets. When Jerome returned, she was still going to be surrounded by straw.

Gritting her teeth, she battled to master a keyboard which required only a feather touch, apparently, to race away in all directions at once, with herself in fruitless pursuit.

The pile of completed pages was still pitifully small when she heard the door behind her open.

She made herself concentrate on what she was doing, as he bent over her. There was no actual, physical contact, yet she was sharply aware of the warmth of his body close to hers, his breath fanning her hair.

Swallowing past her dry throat, Meg risked a swift upward glance, and saw his brows lift. 'Is this all you've done?' His voice was expressionless.

'I'm afraid so.' She gave him an ultra-bright smile, determined to brazen it out. 'I told you I wasn't used to this type of machine.'

'Or any other, it would seem.' There was bite in his tone.

'And I couldn't find a rubber—or any correcting fluid either.'

'Because they're not necessary,' Jerome said with restraint. 'The machine has a built-in correcting tape. You operate it like this.' He demonstrated briefly.

'Oh.' Meg's tone was hollow. 'I see.'

'I hope so.' He paused, reading through one of the pages. 'Your employer is easily pleased, it seems,' he commented grimly.

Meg bit her lip. 'He doesn't complain,' she countered uncomfortably. 'And I—I warned you I wasn't a typist.'

His smile was brief and humourless. 'Clearly your other talents must outweigh your lack of practical skills.' He put the sheet he was scanning down again, holding her gaze with his. He said softly, 'One day, *ma belle*, you must tell me exactly what duties you do perform to deserve your salary.'

She said huskily, 'I don't think that's any of your business.'

'Unless I choose to make it so.' There was sudden harshness in his voice. 'What are you doing, Marguerite, wasting your life in this way? I don't understand you. I could swear you were capable of so much more...'

Meg pushed her chair back, again tautly conscious of his proximity as she got to her feet. She said, 'I'm sorry if I haven't lived up to your expectations.'

'Ah, but this is only the beginning,' Jerome said gently. He put out a hand, and smoothed a strand of hair back from her damp forehead. It was done lightly—even impersonally, but she felt the stroke of his fingers shiver through her bones.

He smiled at her. 'Perhaps tomorrow I can hope for better things.' The words seemed to linger in the air between them, ambiguous, tantalising, offering all kinds of possibilities. Exactly as he intended...

She felt her pulse beat flutter like a bird, with excitement and a kind of absurd hope. But simply recognising the absurdity was her salvation.

Swallowing, she stepped back mentally from some brink. She said, quietly, 'Will you excuse me, please? Tante may need me.'

'At least you fulfil her requirements adequately,' Jerome observed drily.

'That's what I'm here for,' Meg returned, lifting her chin.

'Is it?' The dark eyes flashed at her. 'I hope so, Marguerite. Believe me, I hope so.'

'And what exactly does that mean?' she demanded.

He shrugged. 'I don't want *madame* to suffer any kind of disillusionment.'

She said unevenly, 'She—means a great deal to you, doesn't she?'

'Yes,' he said. 'And not just because of the past, either. I would do a great deal to protect her from distress of any kind.' He paused. 'So be very careful, Marguerite.'

She shook her head. 'I'm not going to hurt her.' She managed a little laugh. 'Incredible as it may seem, I—I care about her too.'

And I envy her, she thought desolately as she went past him, out of the room. At least, when she loved, she was loved in return. I envy her with all my heart.

She spent the time until dinner reading Tante's correspondence to her, helping draft replies, and then writing the letters themselves for Madame de Brissot's signature. She felt a slight awkwardness at being plunged into the deep end of *madame*'s personal affairs like this, but the older woman was entirely matter-of-fact about it, assuring her that it was one of the duties that the absent Madame Aljou took for granted.

But Meg felt miserably guilty as she changed for dinner. It was one thing for *madame*'s own goddaughter to be allowed such a penetrating glimpse of her circumstances, but she herself was a stranger, which made one hell of a difference.

But she now knew for a certainty that none of Margot's optimistic comments about a possible inheritance had any foundation in fact. *Madame*'s income was barely enough for her needs, and her only real asset was the château itself. And where the cash was coming from for all the restoration work heaven only knew. Jerome might have spoken of a labour of love, but the carpenters, electricians, plumbers and masons who'd be needed would hardly regard it in the same light. They'd want to be paid.

But it wasn't her business, let alone her problem, she reminded herself with decision, as she reviewed the selection of clothes in her wardrobe. By the time work started, if it ever did, she'd be long gone and far away.

She dressed with care for dinner, deliberately passing over the honey-coloured dress and the disturbing memories it evoked for the simplicity of a black skirt, teamed with a white silk blouse, high-necked and long-sleeved.

She'd expected *madame* might be down before her, but she found the *salon* empty. Now might be a good chance to call Iris again, she thought restively, picking up the phone and dialling the code for Britain. And this time, with a certain amount of relief, she heard the number ringing out.

'Yes?' Her stepmother's voice was clear but querulous. 'Who is it? What do you want?'

'It's—Margot.' Meg hesitated over the name.

'Margot?' Iris's voice almost squeaked. 'Oh, thank God. I've been nearly going mad. Where are you, darling?'

'Why, France, of course,' Meg said slowly, all her warning antennae on red alert suddenly. 'Madame de Brissot wanted me to let you know I'd arrived safely.'

'Madame de . . .?' Iris sounded bewildered for a moment. 'You mean it's you, Meg? Why the hell didn't you say so, instead of pretending?'

'Because that would be difficult in the circumstances,' Meg returned drily. 'What's happened? What's wrong?'

'You may well ask. It's that damned woman—Steven Curtess's wife.' Iris sounded like the messenger in a Greek tragedy. 'She's left him, for God's sake. Just gone off into the blue, abandoning her children, and making all kinds of damaging statements to the Press,' she added with a little sob of pure indignation.

'I've had the most ghastly people from tabloid newspapers ringing up, wanting to talk to Margot. I had to take the phone off the hook, just for some peace. There've been photographs, headlines about love triangles. It's been a nightmare.

'Margot's had to go into hiding, poor child. And Steven Curtess seems to have had some kind of brainstorm—lost all sense of proportion.' Iris laughed angrily. 'Do you know he had the almighty nerve to come here to this house, bringing his children, insisting that Margot look after them, because there was no one else? Those beastly reporters had an absolute field day over that.

'I told him she wasn't here, but he left them just the same, saying he had to go and look for his wife.' Iris's voice was pure outrage. 'And the children wouldn't stop screaming. I was at my wits' end, until I thought of Nanny Truman. I told her it was an emergency, and she came at once.'

Meg sat down shakily on the arm of the sofa. 'You mean you've still got them?'

'No, no, Nanny took them down to her cottage, thank heaven. But he'll have to make other arrangements. I can't be expected... It's not as if I knew where Margot was, or when she's coming back. Especially after the awful things Corinne Curtess has said about her in the Press. I'm sure half of them are libellous.'

'I doubt that very much,' Meg said wearily.

'That's what my solicitor said when I spoke to him.' Iris gave another sob. 'I'll never be able to hold my head up again after this. And I'm here quite alone, having to bear it all. It was totally selfish of Margot to disappear like this, especially when she must have known what would happen.' She paused. 'You've got to come home, Meg, right away. I need you, to answer the door and telephone, if nothing else.'

'I'm sorry,' Meg said levelly, 'but that's quite impossible. I'm also needed here, and this is where I'm staying. These other problems are none of my making, and I don't want to get involved.'

Iris gasped. 'How can you be so heartless? My nerves are in the most terrible state. I insist that you come back this minute. Have you no sympathy?'

Plenty, Meg thought, as she quietly but firmly replaced the receiver, but all of it was for Corinne Curtess. Although she didn't altogether sound as if she needed it, she thought with a tinge of amusement. Mrs Curtess would undoubtedly be devastated by her husband's adultery, yet launching a pre-emptive strike through the tabloids, and transferring responsibility for the children on to her erring husband and his mistress, was more of a masterstroke than a bid for compassion.

But how typical of Margot to vanish once the going got tough, she thought, her lip curling, although Nanny, kind, sensible and comforting, would be in her element, of course.

'*Bonsoir*.' Jerome was standing, framed in the open French windows, glass of whisky in hand.

So he'd been on the terrace all the time, Meg thought in swift panic. How much had he heard—and what had she said to give herself away? She forced a brief smile as she got to her feet. 'I didn't know you were there.'

'Clearly,' he said laconically, strolling into the room, his dark eyes making a mocking assimilation of her appearance. 'What modesty and discretion,' he commented softly. 'Dare I offer you a drink before you leave for the convent?'

She nodded jerkily. 'Thank you. I'll have a white vermouth.'

'You look as if you need something stronger.' His gaze became more searching. 'I hope there's been—no bad news?'

'On the contrary,' she said, with an attempt at lightness. 'Things couldn't be better.'

And maybe it was true, she thought, as Jerome poured her drink. Perhaps Steven Curtess would come to his senses about his marriage, at last, and Margot be taught a much needed lesson. And soon there'd be some new scandal or sensation, and life would return to something like normality again.

Although it was doubtful if Iris would ever forgive her, she decided, with a mental shrug. But it was time she moved on anyway. From now on, she'd spend every free moment she had in the library, until she'd mastered that monster machine sufficiently to apply for an office job when she got back to Britain. That was the way forward. The only way, she added in silent emphasis, watching Jerome with sudden hopeless hunger as he walked towards her, drink in hand.

She turned away, staring at the glow of the evening sun falling in pools across the terrace flags, terrified that he would read the self-betrayal in her eyes. As he came to her side, she took the glass from him with a murmur of thanks from her taut throat.

'*Santé*.' He lifted his own drink in salute, leaning a shoulder indolently against the frame of the window. Meg, aware of his scrutiny, felt the colour rise in her face, and heard him laugh. 'Again, that incredible blush.'

She couldn't think of a single answer to that, so she continued to stare rigidly in front of her. He was close enough to touch, she realised. If she turned, her arm would brush against him.

'I didn't know grass could be so fascinating,' the tormenting voice went on.

Meg bit her lip. 'I was—thinking about something,' she said lamely.

'But not happy thoughts,' Jerome observed.

He saw far too much, Meg thought bitterly. She hunched a shoulder. 'It's just so quiet here.' She made herself sound faintly resentful. 'And I'm used to city life—things happening all the time.'

'Ah, yes,' he said meditatively. 'Then we shall have to arrange some excitement for you here.'

She tried to ignore the undercurrent of laughter, teasing in his voice. She swallowed some of her vermouth. 'Oh, yes, typing estimates for new roof timbers, no doubt,' she retorted, her tone brittle.

Jerome laughed. 'But even those could be interesting,' he said, 'if you use your imagination to visualise how the house will look when everything is done.'

'Yes, I suppose so,' Meg said slowly, thinking back to the letters she'd written earlier.

Jerome gave her an interrogative glance. 'Is something wrong?'

'No,' she said. 'At least—I just don't understand *why*. Why now, after all this time?' She took a breath, hurrying on, as his brows rose. 'I mean, restoring a house this size is going to cost a small fortune, and what's it all for? There isn't a child— or anyone else to inherit.'

'You think Haut Arignac should just be left to die in peace?'

'No.' Meg hesitated. 'Well, perhaps. After all, who can really afford a home like this any more? And besides, I don't think Tante has that kind of money.'

'And what she has could be put to better use?' There was irony in his voice.

She met his gaze squarely. 'Yes, probably. It's very isolated here, after all, and there must be a lot of sad memories. She could get away—travel ...'

'And forget?'

She moved a hand rather helplessly. 'Well—why not?'

'I don't think it's that simple. Love is not always so transient—so easily dismissed.'

'After all these years?'

'When the love is real,' Jerome said quietly, 'time ceases to matter. An hour or a lifetime become the same.'

Meg's hand tightened round her glass. She said constrictedly, 'And if it turns out to be the wrong person at the wrong time in the wrong place?'

He said harshly, 'Then it's a tragedy. But it doesn't change a thing, *ma belle*, believe me. The wound's as deep, and the scar is eternal.

'And you won't get Madame Marguerite away from here,' he went on after a pause. 'She's spent too much of her life here. In fact, Haut Arignac has become her life, and her love. Now she wishes to pour into it all the accumulated passion of all these sterile years. Would you deny her?'

'No,' Meg acknowledged with a sigh. 'Certainly not when you put it like that.'

'Or are you considering your own interests, perhaps?' His tone of polite interest deceived her at first. But as Meg absorbed the implication in his words her head came round sharply.

'What do you mean?' she demanded.

'*Madame* is frail and lonely,' he said with a shrug. 'Sylvie Aljou, her usual companion, is a good woman, but she has no claim on her affection. Yet already Marguerite is fond of you.'

Meg tensed. 'I already told you,' she said. 'I don't want anything from her.'

His voice hardened derisively. 'I know what you said. But anyone can change their mind. And, in a month, you could achieve a great deal. Even persuade *madame* to divert what resources she has totally in your direction. An old dying house, or a young, lovely woman. I'd say the scales were weighted in your favour, *ma chère* Margot.'

Furiously, her hand swung up, but before she could make contact Jerome seized her wrist in a grip of iron.

'*Ah, non,*' he said softly, and coldly. 'Not now. Not ever.' He jerked her forward, smothering her swift cry of pain with his mouth. He was angry, out of control as never before, his lips parting hers with merciless force, devouring her—ravishing her. And her rage and need matched his, her own demand suddenly as hot, blind and seeking. Hands locked behind his head, Meg gave herself up to the dark, stinging rapture of the moment. Jerome. His name seemed to sing through her veins. Dear God, *Jerome*.

Oblivious to everything, they swayed in each other's arms as if rocked by some high wind, their bodies moulded—welded together.

And then, as suddenly, as violently as it had begun, it was over. Jerome released her, pushing her from him almost with revulsion. He said hoarsely, raggedly, 'Ah, *Dieu*, no. Damn you, Margot, what have you done to me?'

He kicked the fallen whisky glass out of his path, and strode across the *salon* to the door, slamming it behind him.

There was broken glass on the carpet. It was important—imperative that she should clear it up, she thought dazedly. She knelt carefully, gathering the slivers into her handkerchief, wincing as one lacerated her flesh.

She looked down at the bright bead of blood. The wound is deep, she thought, the scarring eternal. And tasted the saltiness of her tears on her bruised mouth.

CHAPTER TEN

THE illuminated dial on her bedside clock said two a.m. Meg stared at it, muttered, 'Oh, hell,' then turned it face downwards.

It had been, she thought, quite the worst evening of her life. She had only just managed to pull herself together, and clear up the mess on the carpet when *madame*, regal in lavender silk, had entered the *salon*.

'So there you are, *petite*.' Fortunately oblivious to Meg's over-bright eyes, and tear-stained cheeks, she seated herself in her usual chair, peering round. 'Jerome is not here yet?'

Meg muttered something indistinguishable.

'Well, it doesn't matter. I am glad to have this chance to see you alone.' Tante opened a drawer in the small table beside her and extracted a shabby velvet box. 'I wish to give you this.'

Meg hesitated, uncomfortably. She began, 'There's really no need...'

'I think there is,' Tante said firmly. 'I've neglected you for far too long.' She pressed the box into Meg's hand. 'Perhaps this will atone for all the years of silence.'

'Oh, no.' Meg was aghast. 'I mean—I didn't come here for this, really...'

'You don't need to tell me that,' Tante said gently. 'Nevertheless, I wish you to have this little token, my dear. Don't deny me this pleasure.'

Swallowing, Meg pressed the catch and opened the box, with acute misgiving. Against the background of yellowing satin, the antique brooch's delicate tracery of amethysts and pearls glowed discreetly.

Meg stared at it, lost for words.

'I hope you like it,' Tante said, at last. 'It has no great intrinsic value, perhaps, but it once meant— so much to me. Now it's yours.'

No need, of course, to ask who had given it to her. Meg said, her voice shaking, 'It's exquisite— the most beautiful thing I've ever seen. But— Tante—I can't take it. You—you don't understand...'

'I think perhaps that I do,' Tante said, her voice gentle. 'You feel Jerome will disapprove.'

'I'm sure he will. He—he doesn't trust me, you see...'

'But that was before he met you.' Tante patted her hand. 'Don't blame him for that, *mon enfant*. He is—over-protective at times, but that isn't such a bad fault, believe me, for a woman to find in a man. And his initial judgement of you was too hasty—based on hearsay. I'm sure he's realised that.'

Meg shook her head. 'On the contrary,' she said quietly. 'I think this would simply confirm all Jerome's worst suspicions.'

'And what do I suspect?' Jerome was standing in the doorway, watching them.

'I have made our dear Margot a small gift,' Tante said. 'But she has scruples about accepting it.'

'How admirably moral,' he drawled.

'So you must tell her that she's being absurd,' Tante ordained sternly.

'With pleasure.' He walked over to Meg, and held out his hand for the box. 'May I see?'

Reluctantly, she surrendered the brooch for his inspection.

'But it's charming,' he said, after a pause. His eyes met hers sardonically, leaving her in no doubt that he'd guessed the brooch's provenance. 'And ideally suited to what you are wearing. Permit me.'

He took the brooch from the box, and pinned it into the silk at Meg's throat, his hand brushing her breast. It was the most fleeting touch, but every nerve of her body reacted in wanton eagerness. She thought rawly, Damn him.

Jerome took a step back. 'The perfect setting,' he said softly.

Dinner seemed endless. As they were going into the dining-room, Jerome was called away by Philippine to the telephone, re-joining them as the soup was being served. Meg, stealing a covert glance at him under her lashes, across the table, discovered a grim set to his mouth and jaw. Whatever message he'd received clearly hadn't pleased him. Perhaps the lady at the *mas* had rung to say she was tired of waiting.

She transferred her attention determinedly to Tante, and began to chat brightly about all she'd seen and done in Albi that morning. From time to time, she was aware of Jerome's cynical gaze resting on her, flickering from her swollen mouth to the gleam of the brooch at her throat, but he made no attempt to intervene in her recital, or introduce an alternative topic of conversation.

'I meant to ask you,' Tante said, when Meg at last paused for breath, 'did you manage to contact your mother?'

'Yes.' Meg sipped some wine. 'I had a—a brief word with her.'

'I hope she is well.' Tante's words were courteous rather than warm. 'She must be missing you.'

Meg gave a constrained smile. 'She's rather too occupied for that at the moment, I think.' She saw

Jerome's eyes narrow suddenly, as he leaned back in his chair, but he made no comment.

Meg had no appetite, and did little but push the food round her plate, making Philippine cluck disapprovingly at her when she cleared away.

When they all adjourned to the *salon*, Tante suggested that Meg and Jerome might like to play backgammon, but Meg declined hurriedly, saying, not altogether mendaciously, that she had a headache.

'And I must also excuse myself.' Jerome took Madame de Brissot's hand and kissed it. 'Something unexpected has cropped up—quite unavoidable, I'm afraid.'

Meg felt her heart skip a beat. So he intended to obey the summons, she thought. Well, what else had she really expected? And it was better this way, she knew, so why did she feel as if she was dying inside?

'You work altogether too hard,' *madame* told him severely. 'Will you be back later?'

'I cannot be sure,' he said, after a pause. 'At any rate, I'll see you in the morning. Sleep well.'

He turned a bleak smile on Meg. 'I hope your headache soon improves,' he told her expressionlessly, and left.

Tante was all concern, offering pain-killers, and Meg was forced to take one to avert suspicion, although it was unlikely to alleviate the real ache in her heart. But she refused to go to bed. The last thing in the world she needed after all was to be on her own to think.

'Such a pity Jerome has been called away,' Tante remarked, adjusting the cushion behind her back. 'It would have rounded your day off nicely if he'd been able to spend the evening.' Her tone was guileless, but Meg wasn't deceived.

She said, 'I came here to be your companion, Tante, not his.'

'But you do begin to like him, don't you, my dear?'

That was a tepid description of the torrent of feeling that had swept her away, Meg thought wrily. She said shortly, 'I haven't really thought about it. Has Philippine brought the paper in?'

'Oh, I don't think I want any news read to me tonight. All wars and death and destruction—so depressing.' Tante pulled a face. 'I'd rather talk about happy things.'

'I'll talk about anything you like,' Meg said gently. 'Except—except Jerome. I—I know how fond you are of each other, and how much you rely on him, but you can't expect me to share in your relationship.'

'Of course not. That would be ridiculous,' Tante said strongly. 'But you can't pretend, either, *ma chère*, that you're not attracted to him, or he to you.' She chuckled. 'When one's sight is reduced, other senses seem to grow stronger, and I've felt this current of emotion that flows between you.'

'He's very good-looking,' Meg said tonelessly. 'Naturally, I'm aware of that...'

'No, no,' Tante said testily. 'I'm talking of something more important and far deeper than just—awareness.'

'I think you're exaggerating,' Meg said desperately. 'Monsieur Jerome and I have only just met.'

'But what a meeting.' Tante's deep chuckle escaped again. 'And how long do you think it takes, foolish child, to *know*...?' She threw back her head. 'Sometimes a look—a word—is all that is necessary—when it's the man who is meant for you above all others.' There was a catch in her voice.

Meg tried to smile. 'It's a very romantic idea, but reality's rather different.'

And what if the man you'd set your heart on didn't share your feelings—or—even worse—wanted you for all the wrong reasons? she asked silently.

'You must not doubt or question love, *ma chère*.' Tante sounded almost stern. 'You should seize it with joy when it's offered, or you could spend your life with nothing but regrets.'

That's something I'm already coming to terms with, Meg thought, biting her lip. Aloud, she said, 'There's no point in even discussing this. You seem to forget I'm only here for a few weeks...'

'On this occasion, perhaps.' Tante patted her hand. 'But now that I've found you again, child, I don't want to lose you. I hope to see far more of you in the future.'

Meg felt choked by guilt. I should never have got into this, she thought wretchedly. Never. A lifetime won't be long enough for all my regrets.

She put up her hand and touched the brooch. The stones felt cold, alien against her fingers. She supposed by right the ornament now belonged to Margot. That was Tante's intention, anyway. But it would fall into her rapacious stepsister's hands over Meg's dead body, although she herself couldn't keep it either. It's just on loan for the duration of my visit, she told herself bleakly. Rather like everything else.

Jerome did not come back, and just after ten o'clock Tante announced her intention of going to bed. Meg read to her for a while from *The Mill on the Floss* then went along to her own room. She detached the brooch with care, then hid the box at the back of a drawer in the dressing-table. It must have cost Tante a lot to part with something so special, she thought sadly. She hadn't bargained for being taken to the older woman's heart quite so fast. Nor had she foreseen that Tante regarded this visit as the beginning of a whole new relationship with her god-daughter.

But that was Margot's problem, not hers, she told herself woodenly, feeling like Judas.

And only one of many, it seemed. Because, now the chips were down, it was apparent that Steven Curtess was opting to try and save his marriage at all costs. Which surely meant that Margot would be out of a job, and out of his life too.

Meg had never had the slightest sympathy with Margot's ruthless pursuit of Curtess, but it occurred to her now, with her newly awakened sensitivity, that if her stepsister was really in love with him, then the loss would destroy her—tear her apart.

Maybe she didn't want to love him, she thought. Perhaps, like me, she couldn't help herself. And she'll suffer for it, as I will, till the end of time.

Sleep proved totally elusive. She lay in the darkness, her mind going in weary circles, but producing no solutions to any of the quandaries which bedevilled her. Finally, she pushed back the covers with determination. So, it was two a.m. She wasn't going to lie here, awake and suffering. She'd use her insomnia for a purpose.

She put on her robe, slid her feet into slippers, retrieved her pocket torch from her travel bag, and opened her bedroom door. Darkness and silence greeted her. Treading carefully, following the thin beam of the torch, she made her way downstairs to the library. She'd face the beast and conquer it, she told herself. It might take her some time to convince Jerome that she wasn't mercenary, but at least she could prove she was competent.

She pushed open the door, and stopped dead, halted in her tracks at the sight of Jerome. The desk lamp was lit, and he was sitting at the table, writing busily. He stared at her as if she were a ghost, then bundled his papers together, pushing them into a folder.

'What are you doing here?' he demanded.

She wasn't going to tell him she'd come down for some secret typing practice. He'd think she'd gone mad.

She temporised. 'I thought I heard a noise.'

'I hope now that your mind is at rest.' Jerome's smile didn't reach his eyes.

'Yes.' She paused. 'I thought you weren't coming back tonight.' The unknown girl must care for him a great deal to be treated in such a cavalier fashion, she thought bleakly.

He shrugged. 'Some of the estimates for the building work were waiting for me at the *mas*. I needed to deal with them. Madame Marguerite is impatient for the work to begin.'

'Yes, of course.' Nervously, Meg tightened the sash of her robe. Jerome observed the gesture with a faint twist of his mouth. He picked up his pen.

'Don't let me detain you,' he said shortly. 'Or is there something else?'

'No—at least . . .' Meg hesitated.

'Well, go on.'

She said in a little rush, 'It's the brooch. I want—I need to explain to you about it.'

Jerome's brows lifted. 'What explanation is necessary? *Madame* wished to make you a gift. It's of no concern to anyone else.'

'I don't think that's true.' Meg touched the tip of her tongue to her dry lips. 'It's an old and lovely piece of jewellery—not a box of chocolates. I tried to tell her I couldn't accept such a thing, but she wouldn't listen.'

His smile was wintry. 'She has become used to her own way in most things. You won't change her in the short time you're here.'

'That's exactly what I'm getting at,' she said. 'I am only here for a little while, and I'll wear the brooch for the duration.' She drew a breath. 'But when I leave I intend to return it.'

Jerome's brows snapped together. 'Return her gift?' He shook his head. 'You couldn't insult *madame* in such a way.'

She said steadily, 'That's why I've decided to return the brooch to you.' She paused. 'After all, it came from your family originally. Didn't it?'

He shrugged again. 'Undoubtedly. If it had been a de Brissot family piece, Henri would have sold it and gambled the proceeds.'

She nodded. 'So I'll just be sending it back where it belongs.'

His frown deepened. 'That is quite unnecessary. The brooch is yours now. Keep it.'

Meg shook her head. 'I can't do that.'

Jerome twisted the pen in his fingers, his dark face sombre. 'Is it because of what I said to you before dinner?' He moved restlessly. 'I had no right...'

Meg lifted a hand. 'There are other reasons too,' she said quietly. 'Please don't ask me to explain.'

'Very well.' He was silent for a moment. 'Is that why you came down here—just to tell me about the brooch?' There was an odd note in his voice.

'I told you—I heard a noise.' Meg was defensive.

'From your room to this?' Jerome asked derisively. 'That's ridiculous.'

Not half as idiotic as the real reason, Meg thought. She said shortly, 'Well, something woke me, anyway.'

'Without doubt,' he said. His tone was bitter, his eyes brooding. 'Probably the same thing, *ma belle*, that's kept me from sleep since our first meeting.' He flung down the pen, and got up, coming round the table towards her.

Meg retreated to the door. She said hurriedly, 'I'm sorry if I've disturbed you. You—you can get back to your work now.'

'Disturbed me?' He gave a short, harsh laugh. '*Dieu*, if that were all. Don't you know what you've done to me, my beautiful, immoral, treacherous little bitch?'

She said shakily, 'How dare you speak to me like that?'

He flung his head back. 'Oh, I dare,' he mocked. 'Because I've been in hell, my lovely Margot. You've turned my life—my plans—into chaos. I know what you are, and it makes no difference. I try to despise you, and I end up wanting you even more.'

He took a step nearer. 'And it's the same for you, *mon amour*. Don't pretend. That's why you're here tonight. Because you can't keep away.' He drew a ragged breath. 'I said I'd make you come to me, and here you are.'

'No.' Meg sobbed the word. 'It's not true. You're crazy...'

'Yes.' He sounded almost meditative. 'Yes, I think I am, a little. My battle was against you, but, God help me, I've ended up fighting myself.'

She said hoarsely, 'I'll go away. I'll tell *madame* I have to go back to England—a family crisis—anything...'

His smile was a travesty. 'Back to your lover—to pick up the pieces, if you can?'

She shook her head wildly. 'I have no lover.'

'No,' he said. 'That is probably the truth, at last. Poor Margot.'

'And don't call me that.' She swallowed. 'Jerome, there are things about me that you have to know.'

'I know them already. Before you ever set foot in France I knew. I intended to take you, to prove that you were worthless—*une petite salope*, who'd belong to anyone.'

'What do you mean?' Meg stared at him in angry incredulity. 'What are you saying?'

'The time for pretence is past, *ma belle*. Now let's be honest with each other.' His voice was harsh. 'I'm caught in my own trap, Marguerite. You've bewitched me too—got under my skin, into my bones.' He paused, his eyes raking her. 'But if I take you maybe I'll be free again, and sane.'

'No.' The word seemed to strangle in her throat. She turned to run, but her foot tangled in the trailing edge of her robe, and she stumbled. In that instant, Jerome caught her. His hands were hard as he pulled her to him—held her crushed in his arms. For a moment she resisted rigidly, fists clenched against his chest. She felt the heated grind of his body against hers through the thin layers that separated them, the supreme male hardness seeking the surcease that only she could offer. Was aware, too, of the small shock-wave of response inside herself, the feminine core of her dissolving, melting ...

As he held her, he began to touch her slowly, as if rediscovering some once familiar journey. His fingertips circled the shape of her face, feathered almost tentatively across temples and cheekbones, outlined the fragile arch of her brows, and the sweet, blunt corners of her mouth.

And, as he did so, the grimness in his own face began to fade, to be replaced by taut yearning, while the hard glitter in his dark eyes steadied to a tingling flame.

'Marguerite.' He spoke her name as if it had been wrenched from some deep wellspring of emotion. And, as if she were turning to the sun, she lifted her face to his.

When he kissed her, it was the merest brush of his lips across hers, yet it tantalised, with a promise of undreamed-of sensation to come. Meg lifted a hand and stroked his cheek, feeling the faint dampness of sweat across the high, powerful bone. She could feel the thud of his heartbeat pulsing through her own body. The raggedness of his breathing was echoed by her own.

His fierce grip had relaxed. Now, it seemed, he was barely holding her at all, and she could choose to go—to walk away—if she wanted. But her legs felt heavy, languorous, her body ached as if it still bore the impress of his, and the blood in her veins was slow and thick, like warm honey.

When she moved at last it was only to put her mouth and, delicately, her tongue against the triangle of warm, hair-roughened skin at the neck of his shirt. She breathed him into her, as if absorbing him through every pore and fibre, luxuriating in the scent, the taste of him, recognising a pleasure that intensified sight and touch.

Jerome began to caress her, his lean fingers tracing the supple length of her spine, and the cleft between her buttocks, before lifting to delineate the smooth curve of her hip, sliding the silky fabric of nightgown and robe against her flesh.

She began to tremble, softly, deliciously. She felt her breasts swell, the nipples hardening into sensuous peaks as Jerome's fingertips whispered across her abdomen, pausing to release the knot of her sash. The robe sighed apart, then fell, pooling round her feet.

He looked at her, his fierce gaze dismissing the thin veil of the nightgown, his face taut with need. A shiver, partly excitement, and partly reaction to the chill of the night air on her overheated skin, ran through her. She tried to control it, but he saw, and his mouth twisted in acknowledgement.

He said softly, 'No, not here—not like this.'

He lifted her into his arms, as if she were a featherweight, and carried her back through the shadowy house to the darkened intimacy of her bedroom.

He put her down on the bed, and leaned across to switch on the lamp. It was like being caught in a spotlight, she thought, lifting a hand to shield her face. Down in the tower room it had all seemed so right—a natural progression of events. But the fact was she'd never been naked in front of a man in her life, and she felt an unexpected wave of shyness engulf her as Jerome slipped down the straps of her nightgown.

She shifted restlessly with a faint murmur of negation. 'Please—the light . . .'

His hands stilled instantly, as his eyes searched her flushed face with wry comprehension. He said, on a little shaken laugh, 'Ah, *Dieu*, Marguerite, don't deny me now, *ma belle*. I have dreamed of you—like this.'

Gently, he freed her breasts from the tiny cups of the bodice, taking their rounded softness into the palms of his hands, cherishing them there as his dark head bent to adore them. Meg's lips parted in a gasp of delight as she felt his mouth suckle each rosy peak, coaxing them to throbbing excitement with the stroke of his tongue. His hands brushed down her body, carrying her nightdress away as if it had been the merest thread of gossamer. His mouth travelled downwards too, planting tiny kisses like a trail of sweet fire. Where he touched, her body blossomed, came to unimagined life.

When his hand eventually parted her thighs, Meg tensed in spite of herself. She was unprepared for the precise sensations which this exploration of her most intimate self would engender.

'*Doucement.*' Jerome's voice soothed her, but she could hear his surprise. 'It's all right, *ma bien aimée*. I won't hurt you.'

He caressed her without haste, every movement of the long fingers a pleasure to be learned and savoured. His eyes never left her face, watching each minute reaction, every flicker of her lashes, every quiver of her parted lips and tiny sobbing sigh which signified her slow, almost bewildered abandonment to delight. She was silk, she was flame, her body opening to him like the unfurling petals of a rose.

His mouth possessed her, his tongue creating tiny whorls of acute sensation. Her mind was empty to everything but this delicate glory of feeling. She searched out blindly into some region of unknowing, and felt her body convulse, implode into rapture.

She floated slowly back to reality, saying his name, reaching for him.

'I'm here,' he told her softly. He took her in his arms, and she felt the warmth of his naked skin against her own. She pressed herself against him, touching him lightly, feverishly, as her hands roved, learning the strength of bone and muscle that created him.

'You're enjoying yourself?' His grin was amused, tender, as he lay back against the pillows watching her under his heavy lids.

'You're beautiful.' Her voice was husky.

'*Du vrai*? I've never been told that before. And you, *ma belle*, look like Eve on the first day of Paradise.'

He drew her hand to his mouth, kissing her fingertips, grazing them softly with his teeth, then guided her with gentle certainty down his body. She was tentative at first, afraid of hurting him as she caressed the proud shaft, only reassured when she heard the first harsh groan of pleasure tear from his throat. Shyly daring, she bent her head, offering him the warm delight of her mouth, feeling his whole body shudder in response, wanting to give him the same release that had been bestowed on her.

Jerome moved restively, his breathing quickening. He said hoarsely, 'Ah, no, my lovely witch,' and lifted her over him, his hands on her hips as he brought her down to join with him.

She hadn't bargained for the pain. Had imagined, in fact, that it was more a myth devised to promote chastity than a physical fact. Now, suddenly, she knew better, and she cried out as her shocked muscles locked in protest against his invasion.

'What's the matter?' Jerome's voice was urgent with astonishment. '*Chérie*, what's wrong?'

Meg sank her teeth into her lower lip. 'I didn't know.' Her voice shook, near to tears. 'I've never...'

Suddenly he was still, staring up at her. 'What are you saying?' His voice grated with sudden harshness. '*Mais, c'est impossible, ça.*'

She felt the first scalding tears on her face. 'I'm sorry—I'm so sorry. Don't be angry with me—please.'

He was silent for a moment, then he said quietly, 'I'm not angry.' He lifted her back gently against the pillows, stroking the hair back from her forehead, wiping the dampness from her cheeks with the edge of the sheet.

Meg lay, eyes closed, one clenched fist pressed against her trembling mouth, aware of the shift of the mattress as he left the bed.

When at last she ventured to look for him, he was standing by the window. He'd pulled on his dark trousers, but his chest was bare. He'd parted the curtains and opened the shutters, and was staring out where the first faint streaks of light had appeared in the eastern sky. In reality, he was only a few feet away, but she felt as if she was looking at him across the distance of the universe.

When he spoke, his voice was almost contemplative. '*Oi deus, oi deus, de l'alba tan tost ve.*' He gave a brief sigh, then turned to her. 'Now,' he said. 'Tell me who you really are.'

CHAPTER ELEVEN

THE silence in the room seemed endless.

'I am waiting.' The quiet voice might have belonged to a stranger. 'Clearly, you are not Margot Trant, so who are you?'

Dry-mouthed, she said, 'Her stepsister. I—I'm Margaret too—Margaret Langtry. I tried to tell you downstairs, but you said—you made me think that you knew...'

'Ah, yes,' he said reflectively. 'But we were at cross-purposes.' He paused. 'And what was the purpose of this masquerade?'

'Margot—couldn't get away. She asked me to take her place.'

'You make it sound so simple,' he said with cold irony. 'Why then did you hide your identity? Pretend to be someone—something—you were not.'

'I can't really explain...'

'Try,' he invited silkily.

She felt icily cold suddenly. She pulled the covers up, hiding her body from his sardonic gaze.

'Margot didn't want her godmother to think she couldn't be bothered.'

'Although it was nothing but the truth.'

'Not altogether. She had strong reasons for not leaving England.'

'Of course,' he said. 'This lover—who never sounded quite real when you spoke of him, for obvious reasons.' He paused. 'The affair had reached a crisis. She did not dare leave, in case he changed his mind in her absence. She needed to be there to hold him—to keep the pressure going.'

'I suppose so.' But, of course, that was exactly how it had been, she thought miserably.

'And you were happy to be her confederate in this?' His contempt grated along her raw nerves. 'You were so eloquent about my grandfather, yet it did not trouble you to help destroy a marriage?'

Meg stared at him. 'You know about that?' she asked, bewilderment mingling with her wretchedness.

'I know,' he said. 'Corinne Curtess is my cousin. We were brought up together, as close as brother and sister. When I saw her last time, it was clear she was deeply distressed about something. Eventually, I made her confide in me.' His smile was grim. 'And that was when I became aware, once more, of Margot Trant.'

'Once more?' Meg queried, shakily. 'Oh, I suppose *madame* had mentioned her to you.'

'*Bien sûr.*' His tone was almost savagely derisive. 'Her god-daughter, the only person approaching a relative whom she possessed—someone she had not seen for many years, because she'd felt no rapport with her as a child. Because she'd seen in her too much of the mother she disliked. Someone to whom, perhaps, she'd been unfair, and should make reparation.

'When Corinne told me about Steven's affair, I prayed for it not to be the same woman. My cousin was convinced that she had no real love for Steven, that she wanted him for ambition—for prestige only. The enquiries I had made only seemed to confirm her fears. No one had a good word to say for Mademoiselle Trant. She was hard, selfish, a gold-digger, concerned only with her own advancement.

'I was as grieved for *madame* as I was for Corinne. I could see her loneliness, could guess why she wanted to be reunited with this girl—to establish a relationship. And I knew that her *petite* Margot was totally unworthy of her.'

'But you didn't say anything. You didn't tell her...?'

'How could I? Corinne had begged me to say nothing about her troubles. She was desperate to save her marriage—convinced that, in time, Steven would come back to her.

'When *madame* decided to invite Margot here, it seemed to me it would kill two birds with one stone. After all, it could only be a matter of time before she betrayed herself in some way—let Madame Marguerite see what she was really like.' His face softened slightly. 'The loss of her sight has given her added perception, in many ways. I relied on that.'

He paused. 'She would also be separated from Steven Curtess. Corinne was sure he was not her only lover, but could get no proof.' His mouth twisted cynically. 'So—I decided to supply it. To establish beyond doubt that she was a tramp, with a penchant for casual affairs by seducing her myself.'

His voice hardened. 'What I did not take into account was *l'inconnue*—the unknown quantity. You.'

His words were like a knife going into her heart. She might have been playing a part, but so had he. Every touch—every kiss—had been a pretence, designed to lure her into self-betrayal. He'd just admitted as much. The lover who'd brought her to rapture in his arms had never existed. Or if he did exist, then he belonged to that other girl at the *mas*—the girl they had both betrayed.

She thought numbly, He didn't even want me. And wished she could die.

She heard him say, 'Why did you do it?' and dragged together the remnants of her pride—her self-respect. Jerome must never know how well he'd succeeded in his cynical, amoral quest, she thought in agony. He must never suspect that she was in love with him.

'I didn't feel I had a choice.' She sounded unutterably weary even to her own ears. 'There's more than one kind of pressure.'

'Without doubt.' His tone was dispassionate. 'You are out of work, of course. That was why you were free to come here, yes? And Margot paid your expenses.'

Her nails dug into the palm of her hands. 'You make it all sound so—mercenary. It wasn't—just that——'

Jerome flung up a hand. 'Oh, spare me the rest.' He was bitterly silent for a moment. 'I should have known that you were a cheat. There were too many discrepancies—your ability to speak French, your failure as a typist—all of it should have told me you were not what you seemed.'

He gestured impatiently at the bed. 'But what made you take the charade so far, you little fool? Did you think you could just—carry off the loss of your virginity?'

Meg bent her head, despair a dull ache inside her. She said tonelessly, 'I suppose—I just didn't realise...'

I let loving you—wanting you—blind me to everything else.

'So—where is your *belle-soeur* now?'

'I've no idea.' Meg hesitated. 'You know, of course, that Corinne has left Steven—and the children?'

'Yes. She wanted to see if drastic action would bring him to his senses. Not that she was happy to leave *les petits* to Margot's tender mercies.'

Meg said shortly, 'She hasn't. The children are with my old nanny and quite safe. And Steven Curtess has gone off after his wife. So her ploy seems to have worked.'

He gave a wintry smile. 'Then everything arranges itself. You, of course, remain the exception.'

She said, off the top of her head, 'I can look after myself. Please don't concern yourself about me.'

'Don't talk like an idiot,' he returned impatiently. 'We cannot leave things as they are. There is so much still that we must discuss...'

'On the contrary, I think you've said more than enough already.' Meg reached down for her discarded nightgown, dragging it over her head, before pushing back the bedcovers. 'Done enough too,' she added with bitter emphasis.

She went to the dressing-table and dragged open the drawer. The velvet jewel case was in her hand as she turned.

'This is the only unfinished business between us,' she said, and threw it to him. 'And that's the end of it. Now get out.' She swallowed, fighting back the tears that threatened to overwhelm her. 'Go back to where you belong, Monsieur Moncourt.'

'Marguerite.' He took a step towards her, and she recoiled.

'No.' She almost shouted the word. 'Just—go. And leave me in peace.'

'Peace.' His laugh was like the cut of a whip. 'Dear God, what peace will there ever be for either of us again?'

She watched his long, lithe stride carry him to the door, and out of her life. She said, again, to the empty room, 'And that's the end of it.' Then she began to cry.

She would have to go away. That was the thought that preyed on her mind as she went mechanically through the morning ritual of bathing and dressing.

She couldn't stay, and put herself through the torture of seeing Jerome each day, knowing that he despised her, remembering those brief ecstatic moments when she'd lain in his arms, and thought that they belonged to each other. What a fool, she thought. What a pathetic lovelorn *idiot*.

Well, she knew better now. And somehow she was going to have to face Madame de Brissot. Her secret was out now, with a vengeance, and she owed it to Tante to tell her the truth before Jerome did.

But that wasn't an immediate ordeal. *Madame* breakfasted in her room, and she would wait to talk to her until she came down to the *salon*, she decided. It would have to be done, although she could imagine the probable reaction, she thought, setting her teeth. *Madame* would not relish being imposed upon. She could only hope that Jerome hadn't got there first.

But when she got downstairs she learned from Philippine that Jerome wasn't there—that he'd gone off in his car more than two hours earlier.

'Driving,' Philippine added with severity, 'like the wind.'

'Oh.' Meg was taken aback. 'Did he say when he'd be returning?'

Philippine shrugged. 'He was displeased,' she said. 'Therefore one does not ask unnecessary questions.'

Meg made her reluctant way to the library. She needed to retrieve her robe before the girl from the village who helped with the cleaning got to it first. She folded it up neatly but it was still too bulky to fit into the pocket of her jeans, and she balked at the idea of carrying it back to her room in plain view. Philippine's button eyes were far too shrewd.

She glanced round the room, the breath catching in her throat. She found she was going over in her mind everything Jerome had said to her. He'd accused her of bewitching him. 'I'm caught in my own trap...' She could almost hear his voice echoing back at her from the walls. 'I try to despise you, and I end up wanting you even more.'

But it was useless trying to dredge some morsel of hope from any of that, she told herself desolately. Because it wasn't desire she craved from Jerome but love. And, in his eyes, she was just as bad as Margot, if not worse. Quite apart from the fact that he belonged to someone else. Something he chose to ignore. But she could not.

Her best move would be to go back to her room and pack. Then, when *madame* asked her to leave, she'd at least be prepared, she decided.

She saw the document wallet still lying on the table where Jerome had left it the night before. She'd borrow that to put her robe in. As she emptied the papers it contained on to the table, a few of them fluttered to the floor. Meg looked them over casually as she picked them up. As he'd said, they were estimates from local artisans—carpenters, masons and plumbers, and Meg whistled in dismay as she saw the amounts they were asking. How could Tante afford anything approaching that kind of money? she asked herself.

As she sorted them into a pile, she saw the same letterheads recurring, and realised that some of the estimates appeared to be in duplicate. Presumably Jerome intended Madame de Brissot to have one copy, while he retained the other for his records, she thought.

She put the two tenders from Mauristand et Fils side by side, then stopped, her brows snapping together. The work being estimated for was exactly the same in both, but the amounts quoted couldn't have been more different. One of the estimates was asking for hundreds of thousands of francs less than the other. And a hundred thousand francs was roughly worth a thousand pounds, Meg thought numbly.

She compared the rest, aware that her hands were trembling, and that there was a sick feeling in the pit of her stomach. The disparity was more or less the same in all of them.

She sank down on to the chair. No, she thought frantically. It's not possible. It can't be.

She found the sheet Jerome had been working on, remembering how he'd pushed it out of sight as she entered, and said, 'Madame Marguerite is impatient for the work to begin.'

So impatient, she thought, swallowing, and so trusting that she'd accept any figure without question from the grandson of the man she'd loved. And when the money had been handed over the firms concerned would do the work at a cut rate, and Jerome would share the profit with them. It wasn't a novel idea, by any means, but Madame de Brissot would suspect nothing, because it was Jerome—*Jerome*.

Disillusion rose in her throat, bitter as gall. And he'd dared to take the moral high ground against her. Her pretence seemed innocent by comparison, she thought, pushing the papers away from her in disgust. He'd dared call her a cheat. Well, he was a cheat too—a two-timer—but this was fraud—and perpetrated against an old half-blind woman whom he claimed to love and respect.

Meg's hands clenched impotently into fists. Hypocrite, she accused silently. Thief. He couldn't be allowed to get away with it. She'd drive to the *mas* right now and confront him, and his woman, threaten to expose him to *madame* and to the police unless he suppressed the false estimates.

She thrust the papers back into the wallet, and made for her room, leaving her robe on the table. That would have to wait, she thought grimly. She was crossing the hall on the way to the stairs when the front door swung open, filling the hall with sunlight. And in the midst of it was Jerome.

He looked preoccupied, his face tired and drawn, and in spite of everything Meg's heart turned over at the sight of him. You stupid fool, she adjured herself with contempt.

He checked at the sight of her. 'I hoped I would see you,' he said quietly. 'We need to talk.'

'I couldn't agree more,' Meg's voice bit. 'I suggest somewhere we won't be overheard.'

He saw the document wallet, and his face hardened. 'I came to fetch that. What are you doing with it?'

'Let's discuss it in private.' Meg led the way into the dining-room and closed the heavy door. She took out the two sets of papers and slapped them down, side by side, on the gleaming surface of the big table. 'And what percentage do you get, Monsieur de Moncourt?'

His brows lifted in hauteur. 'What do you mean?'

'I mean swindling an elderly woman out of money she can't afford anyway,' she flung at him. 'Tante thinks the sun and moon shines out of you, Jerome, and you're taking her for a ride—fiddling her rotten—you and these others.' Her voice rose passionately. 'And you *dare* talk to me about deceit.'

His mouth tightened. He took a step towards the table. 'Have you shown her those estimates?'

'Not yet.' Meg put herself between him and the precious papers.

He halted, his expression faintly derisive as he studied her defiant stance. 'Thank God for that at least.'

She stared at him. 'Is that all you have to say?'

'You're waiting for me to make some excuse—to defend myself?' He shook his head, smiling crookedly. 'No, *ma belle*. Think what you choose.'

'And if I take these to *madame*?'

'I can't stop you,' he said. 'But I hope that you won't. It would cause me—problems.'

'You deserve to have problems.' Her voice shook. 'You deserve to go to gaol for the rest of your life. *Madame* trusted you because of your grandfather, and you—you traded on that—wormed your way into her confidence—her affection. You're despicable.'

'Have you finished?' He was very pale, and a tiny muscle jerked beside his mouth.

'I've barely started. How could you do it, Jerome? How could you treat her like this? You can't need the money.' She spread out her hands beseechingly. 'Make me understand.'

His voice was quiet ice. 'I think that is impossible. And why should you want to, anyway?'

Because I love you, her heart cried out to him. Because this contradicts everything I believed about you. Because my dream is broken, and I want it mended.

Slowly, she bent her head. 'There's no reason.'

'Then may I have my papers, together with a guarantee that you won't meddle in this matter?'

Something inside her seemed to die. She said dully, 'To use your own words—I can't stop you. But I won't keep quiet. *Madame* has treated me with nothing but kindness, and I won't repay her by allowing her to be defrauded like this.'

'Go to her, then. See if she believes you.'

Meg bit her lip. 'But I don't want her to be hurt either, and she would be—desperately.' She paused. 'There is an alternative.'

'How enterprising of you, *ma chère*.' The hooded eyes were coldly sardonic. 'Are you going to tell me about it?'

She said, 'I want you to give up the project. Make some excuse to *madame*, and let her find someone else—another architect.'

'And what happens to me? Do I simply disappear—retreat back to Paris like my grandfather?' He shook his head. 'No, I don't think Octavien could survive another defection.'

'You'll think of something. But in future it might be best—kinder to *madame*—if you kept away from the château altogether.'

'You have it all worked out.' His mouth curled. 'But I'm afraid your plan won't work. Because I have no intention of shunning Haut Arignac, now or at any time to come. Nor would *madame* wish me to.'

'Not if she knew the truth about you?'

'Point the finger,' he said. 'Tell her your suspicions. She may be a little upset, but it won't last.'

She said thickly, 'Your arrogance is unspeakable.'

He shrugged. 'She has more faith in me than you do, *ma belle*, that's all. But at least we have no illusions about each other, you and I.'

He walked past her, swept the papers together, and replaced them in the wallet. 'With my compliments,' he said, and put it into her hands with a little bow.

She stared up at him, her wide eyes enormous in her pale face. 'Is—that all?'

'Except for this,' said Jerome, and took her in his arms. His kiss was deep, and without mercy, as if he was trying to burn his way into her consciousness forever. Somehow, she found the strength to endure it—and, when it was over, to watch him walk away without a backward glance.

* * *

'Was that Jerome's car I heard a little while ago?' Madame de Brissot asked when, her packing done, Meg eventually joined her on the terrace.

'Yes.' Meg's voice was constrained. She might have no more illusions, as he'd said, she thought wretchedly, but how did she begin to tell this woman who loved him like a son that he was little better than a common thief?

She sat down on one of the wicker chairs and put the incriminating wallet on the small table between them.

'He must have been in a great hurry,' Tante mused. 'He brought you some more typing, perhaps.' She laughed gently. 'He is even keener than I am to see this work started, but that's understandable.'

'It's not more typing.' Meg took tentative hold of the bull's horns. 'It's some of the estimates for the restoration. I thought maybe you should see them.'

'Well, that is thoughtful.' Tante sounded surprised. 'But Jerome has already discussed them with me.' She smiled. 'He brought up my breakfast tray this morning, as he often does when he spends the night here, and went through the figures then.'

'He did?' Meg swallowed. 'But he left them with me, or I thought...' She paused, then plunged on. 'Were they—satisfactory?'

'Far better than I'd dared to hope.' *Madame* delved into the tapestry bag hanging from the arm of her chair, and produced a folded paper. She handed it to Meg. 'See for yourself, *petite*.'

Meg saw. The figures listed in Jerome's unmistakable writing were all the lower ones.

'You're—sure these are right?' she asked hesitantly.

'Yes, Jerome offered to show me the actual quotations, but I begged him to spare me.' She leaned back against her cushions contentedly. 'When my share of the restoration is paid for, I shall be quite comfortably off. I shan't know myself.'

'Your share?' Meg's voice was hollow. 'I don't quite understand. You mean you're not paying for this renovation?' She caught herself. 'I'm sorry. I shouldn't be asking this. It's—it's none of my business.'

Madame shrugged. 'But why should I mind?' she said. 'It isn't really a secret, and you are almost family after all. I'm paying a proportion of the cost, *mon enfant*. Jerome didn't want me to pay anything at all, but I insisted. In fact, I made it a condition of the sale.'

'Sale?' Meg echoed, her head reeling.

Madame nodded. 'The papers will be signed at the end of the week. And Haut Arignac will finally belong to Jerome.' She smiled. 'My first dream come true.'

Meg smiled back weakly. No dream for her, she thought, but an actual living nightmare in full Technicolor with stereophonic sound.

She'd jumped to all kinds of conclusions, accused Jerome quite falsely, said terrible things—unforgivable things—to him. And he hadn't bothered to defend himself. He could have corrected all her misapprehensions so easily, but he hadn't cared sufficiently to do so. Because her opinion of him didn't matter. That was the sombre truth of it all. It was immaterial to Jerome whether she loved him or loathed him, and he could have given her no more positive proof of his total indifference, she thought miserably.

Madame leaned forward and patted her hand. 'And I still have other hopes,' she said.

Meg looked down at her tightly clasped hands. 'I'm afraid they're doomed to disappointment,' she said quietly.

Madame pursed her lips. 'I thought dear Jerome was quite *distrait* when he visited me this morning. I hope you two haven't been quarrelling?' She peered at Meg. 'Are you wearing your brooch today?'

Meg glanced down at her simple cotton shirt. 'Not with these clothes.' She hesitated. 'Tante— *madame*—there's something you should know...'

'What is it, *ma chère*?'

Meg took a deep breath, nerving herself, only to be interrupted by the sudden arrival of Philippine pattering on to the terrace.

'*Pardon, madame—mademoiselle*——' her rosy face was unusually solemn as she looked from one to the other '—but a visitor has called.'

'I was expecting no one.' Madame de Brissot paused. 'Has this visitor a name?'

'*Oui, madame.*' Philippine's worried expression deepened, and her eyes flickered towards Meg in obvious embarrassment. 'She says she is Mademoiselle Trant—Mademoiselle Margot Trant.'

CHAPTER TWELVE

THE silence was deafening. Meg, flushing to the roots of her hair, tried desperately to think of something to say, and failed miserably.

'But how interesting,' *madame* commented. 'Please ask her to join us, Philippine, and bring coffee.'

As Philippine disappeared on her errand, Meg said urgently, '*Madame*—you've got to let me explain...'

'Later, *mon enfant*.' *Madame* adjusted her dark glasses and turned her face towards the French windows.

A moment later, Margot appeared through them, and stood, framed dramatically. She looked incredibly confident and glamorous in crisp white trousers with a matching shirt in heavy silk. A bronze leather belt circled her slim waist, and her sandals and capacious shoulder-bag were in the same colour.

Clearly, Meg thought drily, in spite of her state of shock, Margot had forgotten she'd just be a blur and gone for effect.

'Tante.' Margot came gracefully up to the chair and dropped a kiss a few millimetres to the left of *madame*'s cheek. 'Oh, this is wonderful. Had you quite given me up?' She looked round inhaling ecstatically. 'Blissful fresh air. How anyone can prefer cities...' Her gaze came to rest on her frozen stepsister. 'Hi, Meg.' She dropped prettily on to one knee beside *madame*'s chair. 'I hope you didn't mind Meg filling in for a few days for me. Such a nuisance, my leave of absence being delayed like that. I hope she explained it all to you?'

'Is that how it was?' *madame* asked. 'I see.'

'You mean she didn't tell you?' Margot turned a shocked look on Meg. 'Darling, you are dreadful. What on earth were you thinking about? Not that it matters, I suppose. I'm here now.' She took another sweeping look round.

'So who precisely is this other young woman I've had the pleasure of entertaining?' There was a note of chilled steel in *madame*'s voice.

Meg got to her feet. She said quietly, 'I'm Margaret Langtry, *madame*, Margot's stepsister.'

'Meg's out of work, so I thought a break in France might do her good,' Margot added brightly. 'But she's desperate to go off and look for bits of dead Cathar or something, aren't you, sweetie?' She turned back to *madame*. 'Meg's last job was in an old bookshop, so she's heavily into mouldering remnants of history.'

'Which is possibly why she's fitted in here so well,' *madame* said drily.

'Well, I'm glad she's made herself useful.' Margot lowered her voice conspiratorially. 'In the beginning, she wasn't at all keen to come, you know.'

'You amaze me,' said *madame*. 'Ah, here is the coffee. Perhaps—Meg, is it?—would like to perform one last duty as my companion, and pour it for us.'

Meg, stunned at first, but growing angrier by the second, would have preferred to up-end the coffeepot and its contents over Margot's exquisitely windblown blonde head, but she complied in brittle silence. Her stepsister was deliberately making her sound like some indigent poor relation, she realised furiously—and as if assuming her identity had been some private idea of her own.

Margot drew her chair up beside *madame*'s and began to chat vivaciously. For someone who'd just been jilted by the man she loved, she appeared in good form, but Meg detected a certain fixity in her blue eyes, and lines of strain and discontent round her mouth.

Livid at Steven Curtess's defection she might be. Heartbroken she certainly wasn't. She'd suffered a reverse, but she'd soon be back, clawing her way to the top again. And, in her version, of course, it would be Steven Curtess who'd lost out.

Meg swallowed her coffee past the lump in her throat. And she, it appeared, was going to be a loser too. Margot had got her story in first with the utmost skill, and there was no way now in which she could explain to *madame* why she'd practised such a deception, or make amends for it.

'Would you excuse me?' she asked, as Margot eventually paused for breath. 'I have my packing to see to.' She hesitated. 'After all, there's no reason for me to remain here any longer.' The words felt as if they'd been wrenched out of her.

'None at all.' *Madame*'s expression was remote. 'There is a taxi service in Arignac. If you ask Philippine, she will telephone them for you. Shall we say half an hour?'

Meg nodded tautly. 'Thank you.'

Aware of Margot's gaze following her, she held her head high as she left the terrace, but her legs were shaking under her. The reprieve she'd prayed for had not been granted, but what else could she reasonably have expected in the circumstances? Madame de Brissot was obviously deeply offended, and who could blame her?

She relayed the message about the taxi to Philippine who was clearly bursting with suppressed curiosity, collected her robe from the tower room, then went upstairs.

In a way, she had to be glad that she wouldn't be spending another night there, she thought, averting her gaze determinedly from the big bed. It held too many associations—searing and poignant— Jerome's hands on her body, Jerome's kisses on her mouth.

She shut down the images in her mind with a little gasp of pain. Concentrate on practicalities, she told herself—and there were enough of them. She supposed, counting the money she had left, that she'd better get the taxi to take her to Albi, and then find some form of public transport to Toulouse. She had the return half of her flight ticket, which presumably she could change for an earlier plane, even if it meant going on stand-by.

With a sigh she tucked the ticket and her passport into her bag.

'Make sure you don't leave anything behind,' Margot said from the doorway. She strolled in, wrinkling her nose expressively as she looked around.

'If this is the guest room, God knows what the rest can be like,' she remarked disparagingly. 'But beggars can't be choosers, I suppose. And it's somewhere to hole up until the dust settles.' She glanced at Meg. 'I suppose you've heard about my little local difficulty?'

'Yes,' Meg said levelly. 'But I hardly expected you to show up here, as a result.'

Margot shrugged. 'Where better?' she retorted insouciantly. 'Did you know that bitch had sicked her ghastly kids on to us? Talk about the ultimate revenge.'

'Except that Nanny seems to be bearing the brunt of it all.' Meg paused. 'And speaking of that, where does this leave our agreement about the cottage?'

Margot yawned. 'God, you can be boringly obsessive sometimes. Let it stand. Who cares?'

'I do,' Meg said harshly. 'In fact I care about a lot of things. Your godmother, for instance, and this house for another.'

Margot pulled a face. 'Both crumbling into extinction as far as I can see. I thought the old girl had money.'

She's going to have, Meg thought grimly. You've come at just the right time.

She said, 'Nevertheless, it's been the nearest thing to a home I've had for a long time.'

'Don't be ridiculous,' Margot snapped. 'You only just got here.'

'It doesn't always take forever to discover that you belong,' Meg said. To a place, or a person, she thought with a pang of sheer yearning. Sometimes a day, or even an hour. But in her case it had been the wrong time, the wrong place, and definitely the wrong man from the very start. She should never have got involved even marginally. Now she had to go home, and, somehow, put the pieces of her life back together again.

Philippine tapped on the door. 'Your taxi is here, *mademoiselle*. And *madame* is waiting to wish you goodbye in the *salon*.'

'Then I'll leave you to it, and have a look round,' Margot said. She hunched a shoulder. 'What the hell do they do for night life round here?'

Meg carried her bags down to the hall, where the driver, a short man with a drooping moustache, was waiting to stow them in his cab. Then, reluctantly, she went into the *salon*. *Madame* was standing by the empty hearth, her hands folded in front of her, her face remote and unsmiling. The pose was studiedly formal. Lady of the house dismissing unsatisfactory employee, Meg thought unhappily.

She said quietly, 'I wish to thank you, *madame*, for all your kindness to me.' She lifted her chin. 'I'm sorry I—misled you as I did. And I wish I could have told you about it myself.'

'I think too little can be said on the matter.' It was the *grande dame* speaking. She held out her hand. 'A pleasant journey, Miss Langtry.'

Meg clasped her fingers, searching in vain for some softening in the older woman's face. She said, 'I—I haven't kept the brooch you gave me. I restored it to Monsieur Moncourt. I hope you don't mind?'

Madame nodded. 'That was probably the best course.' She released Meg's hand and turned away with a kind of finality.

Meg murmured something and got herself out of the room. Philippine was waiting at the front door, and Meg found herself engulfed in a hearty embrace.

'Don't look so sad, little one. Everything arranges itself in time.' Philippine produced a flat package from her overall pocket with the air of a conjuror. '*Madame* told me to give you this.'

'I think there must be some mistake.'

'No, no.' Philippine shook her head vigorously, and thrust the package into Meg's unwilling hands. 'It is for you. You must take it. *Au revoir.*'

Meg forced a smile. '*Adieu*, Philippine.'

She didn't look back as the taxi drove away. She couldn't believe how quickly it had all happened. But that had been the pattern of life ever since she'd arrived in the Languedoc—a series of lightning changes. From sunshine to storm, she thought. Passionate love, and passionate hate. And I can't say I wasn't warned.

She settled back in her corner and looked down at the package she was still holding. She hoped it wasn't money. That in some weird way would be the ultimate ignominy—worse than being practically turned off without a character, she thought wrily.

She tore off the wrapping paper, and stiffened in disbelief. It was *madame*'s poetry book. She opened it at the flyleaf and read again the faded inscription. 'To Marguerite. My whole heart. J.'

Oh, she thought, but how could she bear to let it go, after all this time—and how can I bear to keep it?

She began to flick through the pages, and the book fell open as if at an accustomed place. The opening line, with its quaint spelling, seemed to glow up at her once more. '*Ma doulce amour, ma plaisance chérie,*' she read, before it was blurred under a mist of tears. 'My sweet love,' she thought, 'My source of all delight.'

Perhaps *madame* had known that words on a page were all that she too would have to remember, and had made sure they were the right words.

Not an *aubade*, of course. But how could there ever be another?

She was startled out of her reverie by a sharp blast on the taxi's horn, and a muttered expletive from the driver. 'This species of imbecile,' he addressed the world at large. 'What does he think he's doing?'

Looking past him, Meg became aware of a car totally blocking the road in front of them. There must have been some kind of accident—a tyre blow-out maybe—for it to end up at that angle, she thought, hoping that no one was hurt.

And then she recognised the car. Carefully she closed the book, aware that the palms of her hands were suddenly damp, and shrank back into her seat, as if willing herself to be absorbed into its worn upholstery and vanish.

The car door was pulled open. '*Nous retournons à zero*,' Jerome remarked, almost casually, over a stream of invective from the driver. 'Back to square one. Where we began, *ma belle*. Out you get, before more traffic arrives.'

Meg glared at him. 'I'll do nothing of the kind.'

His brows lifted. 'You wish to be carried yet again?' He turned to the incensed driver, said something quiet which Meg couldn't translate, and handed him some money.

Meg, scrambling into the road, saw her bags being unloaded from the boot.

'What are you doing? Leave them there.' She stamped her foot.

The driver shrugged. In view of such largesse, she was given to understand, *monsieur* was free to block the road and hijack his passengers until the seas ran dry. He gave Jerome an approving wink, kissed his hand at the sky, reversed into a convenient gateway and drove off.

Meg's hands clenched into fists. 'What the hell do you think you're doing?'

'Taking you home.' Jerome tossed her luggage into his boot and slammed it shut.

'To England?' This was being seen off the premises with a vengeance.

'I'd hoped to the *mas*—if you can begin to think of that as home. The château, of course, remains Marguerite's for her lifetime.' He looked at her with that slanting smile which twisted her heart. 'Well, can you make a life with me at Goncaud?'

The sun was warm gold. In the thick grass at the side of the road, cicadas were whirring. A breeze stirred the trees, bringing with it a scent of ripe fruit.

She said, 'No,' and, helplessly, 'This is crazy.'

He opened the passenger door of his car, and Meg got in. She didn't really have an alternative now that the taxi had gone, and maybe, when Jerome had recovered from his brainstorm, he'd drive her to Albi.

She said, 'How did you happen to be here?'

'Madame Marguerite telephoned the *mas* and told me you were leaving, and the time of your taxi.

I gambled that he'd bring you this way. Otherwise I intended to blockade the airport at Toulouse.'

For a maniac, he sounded quite reasonable. Except for what he was saying. She said, '*Madame* told you? But that's impossible. She's just thrown me out.'

He said patiently, 'She thought it would be better for you to be with me—until she has had time to deal with Margot.' He flicked a smile at her. 'You are not the only one who can play a part, *ma belle*.'

She was silent for a moment, then she said in a small voice, 'I know what you did with those estimates—and why.'

'I hope you did not share your knowledge with *madame*? She has great pride. She would think I was offering charity.'

'But it isn't,' she said slowly. 'If everything had worked out and she'd married your grandfather, he'd have made sure she was happy and comfortable always. You're just—repairing the damage.'

He said gently, 'You understand. I knew you would.'

Meg bit her lip. 'But you couldn't know,' she protested. 'Not after I'd misjudged you so dreadfully—said all those terrible things.'

'Perhaps I deserved them,' he said. 'For misjudging you, and saying so many more terrible things myself.'

'But I did pretend I was Margot,' she said. 'Nothing can alter that. Whereas you were only guilty of kindness.'

Jerome pulled the car on to a place where the verge widened, and stopped the engine.

'I was not very kind to you, *mon ange*,' he said softly. 'I thought it would be so easy to hate you, for what you had done to Corinne. She's so warm, so gentle, and she loves her husband so much.' He shrugged. 'Although none of our family can understand why. Then I met you, and there was something—some spark I've never known before. I knew I couldn't let you slip away out of my life, and then I saw the name on your luggage.'

He shook his head. 'I think it was the worst moment of my life—to admit to myself that I'd been attracted to the little bitch who was trying to ruin my cousin's life.

'I told myself I'd be just as cold-blooded in my pursuit of you. But every time I came near you, touched you, it seemed to tear me apart. I wanted to take you without mercy, and cherish you for the rest of my life, all at the same time.'

'I don't see anything wrong with that,' Meg said demurely.

'Oh, *là*.' His smile was warm and sensuous as he stroked a finger down the curve of her cheek. 'I shall remind you of that tonight.'

'I hope so.' Her eyes met his with candour, nothing hidden, least of all her sheer physical enrapturement with him.

'And this time I shall treat you with the gentleness you deserve,' he promised. 'I should have known from the first you were not Margot.' He took her hand, caressing her fingertips with his lips.

'Because I'm a lousy typist?' she teased.

He laughed. 'No—everything you said—everything you did. But I silenced my doubts—saw only what I wanted to see.' His mouth twisted remorsefully. 'Last night, I should have realised you were untouched. And when I knew beyond question that you were a virgin, and could not be Margot, I got angry—but angry with myself for being a blind, insensitive fool. And, *hélas*, the anger rubbed off on you.'

He groaned. 'At the moment when we should have been learning how to love we were screaming at each other.' He looked at her gravely. 'Couldn't you have trusted me with the truth before then, Marguerite?'

'I wanted to, so much.' She took a breath. 'But I wasn't the only person involved. Margot had blackmailed me into coming. They were threatening to sell my old nanny's cottage and force her into a home, unless I agreed.' She frowned. 'In fact it could still happen. I don't trust Margot, or Iris for that matter.'

'She is very old, this nurse, and infirm, perhaps?'

'Indeed, she isn't,' Meg said strongly. 'Otherwise she couldn't be looking after your cousin Corinne's children at this minute.'

'Then it might please her to live in France and look after our babies, when they come.'

Tears pricked at her eyelids. 'I think she'd love it. Oh, *Jerome*.'

'Of course,' he said softly. 'It all depends on one small point—that you love me as I love you. You haven't said so yet. And, maybe, for you it's too soon.'

'No,' she said. 'It's not too soon. And how strange that we can both be so sure.'

'We're not the only ones,' he said drily. '*Madame* was sure from the first. I must telephone her as soon as we get to the *mas* and let her know you are safe with me, and not waiting for some plane to England.'

'I hope she'll be pleased.' Meg wrinkled her brow. 'She was very chilly when I left.'

'She was anxious for you to leave. She could sense that Margot's arrival had added to your tension and unhappiness.' He grimaced slightly. 'She was not pleased with me this morning when I told her what a mess I had made of everything.'

Meg worked this out. 'So, when I saw her later, she already knew I wasn't Margot?'

He nodded. 'She said, like me, she had always known. That the spoiled ill-tempered child could not have grown into a girl of such quiet grace.' He glanced at his watch. 'By now I think Mademoiselle Trant will have left the château, sadder perhaps and wiser, though I doubt it. And my guests will also have left the *mas*. I hope they don't meet on the road.'

'Your guests?' Meg gasped. 'You mean Corinne? Then it was her that I saw...'

'You have sharp eyes.' Jerome sounded amused. 'Her husband is with her now. She telephoned the *mas* that first evening we were together to say she was on her way. He joined her yesterday. That was the phone call I took at dinner. They are now heading for Paris to continue their second honeymoon in my apartment there.'

Meg digested this. 'But how in the world did he know where to find her?'

'He knew,' Jerome said simply. 'As I knew just now. Which gives me hope for their future together. Although I am more interested in ours.' He kissed her gently, but very completely. 'Will you be my wife, Marguerite, and share the storms and the sunlight with me?'

'Yes,' she said, and her mouth trembled into a smile. '*"Ma doulce amour, ma plaisance chérie."* And will you show me another dawn?'

'Every morning of our lives,' he said huskily. 'Now let's go home.'

As he started the car, she said, 'There's one problem, Jerome. What are we going to do about Octavien? When do you think he'll stop calling me *Anglaise*?'

He laughed. 'Probably, *mon amour*, at our son's christening.'

And he was right.

Hi—

I'm in trouble—I'm engaged to Stuart, but I suddenly wish my relationship with Jan Breydel wasn't strictly business. Perhaps it's simply the fairy-tale setting of Bruges. Belgium is such a romantic country!

Love, Geraldine

This June, Harlequin invites
you to a wedding of

Promised Brides

Celebrate the joy and romance of weddings past with
PROMISED BRIDES—a collection of original historical short
stories, written by three best-selling historical authors:

The Wedding of the Century—MARY JO PUTNEY
Jesse's Wife—KRISTIN JAMES
The Handfast—JULIE TETEL

Three unforgettable heroines, three award-winning authors!
PROMISED BRIDES is available in June wherever Harlequin
Books are sold.

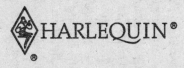

HARLEQUIN®

PB94

Harlequin Books requests the pleasure of your company this June in Eternity, Massachusetts, for WEDDINGS, INC.

For generations, couples have been coming to Eternity, Massachusetts, to exchange wedding vows. Legend has it that those married in Eternity's chapel are destined for a lifetime of happiness. And the residents are more than willing to give the legend a hand.

Beginning in June, you can experience the legend of Eternity. Watch for one title per month, across all of the Harlequin series.

HARLEQUIN BOOKS... NOT THE SAME OLD STORY!

Relive the romance....
Harlequin is proud to bring you

A new collection of three complete novels every month. By the most requested authors, featuring the most requested themes.

Available in May:

Three handsome, successful, unmarried men are about to get the surprise of their lives.... Well, better late than never!

Three complete novels in one special collection:

DESIRE'S CHILD by Candace Schuler
INTO THE LIGHT by Judith Duncan
A SUMMER KIND OF LOVE by Shannon Waverly

Available at you're retail outlet from

HARLEQUIN®

Don't miss these Harlequin favorites by some of our most distinguished authors!
And now, you can receive a discount by ordering two or more titles!

HT #25551	THE OTHER WOMAN by Candace Schuler	$2.99	☐
HT #25539	FOOLS RUSH IN by Vicki Lewis Thompson	$2.99	☐
HP #11550	THE GOLDEN GREEK by Sally Wentworth	$2.89	☐
HP #11603	PAST ALL REASON by Kay Thorpe	$2.99	☐
HR #03228	MEANT FOR EACH OTHER by Rebecca Winters	$2.89	☐
HR #03268	THE BAD PENNY by Susan Fox	$2.99	☐
HS #70532	TOUCH THE DAWN by Karen Young	$3.39	☐
HS #70540	FOR THE LOVE OF IVY by Barbara Kaye	$3.39	☐
HI #22177	MINDGAME by Laura Pender	$2.79	☐
HI #22214	TO DIE FOR by M.J. Rodgers	$2.89	☐
HAR #16421	HAPPY NEW YEAR, DARLING by Margaret St. George	$3.29	☐
HAR #16507	THE UNEXPECTED GROOM by Muriel Jensen	$3.50	☐
HH #28774	SPINDRIFT by Miranda Jarrett	$3.99	☐
HH #28782	SWEET SENSATIONS by Julie Tetel	$3.99	☐

Harlequin Promotional Titles

#83259	UNTAMED MAVERICK HEARTS (Short-story collection featuring Heather Graham Pozzessere, Patricia Potter, Joan Johnston)	$4.99	☐

(limited quantities available on certain titles)

	AMOUNT	$
DEDUCT:	10% DISCOUNT FOR 2+ BOOKS	$
	POSTAGE & HANDLING	$
	($1.00 for one book, 50¢ for each additional)	
	APPLICABLE TAXES*	$ _____
	TOTAL PAYABLE	$ _____
	(check or money order—please do not send cash)	

To order, complete this form and send it, along with a check or money order for the total above, payable to Harlequin Books, to: **In the U.S.:** 3010 Walden Avenue, P.O. Box 9047, Buffalo, NY 14269-9047; **In Canada:** P.O. Box 613, Fort Erie, Ontario, L2A 5X3.

Name: _____

Address: _____ City: _____

State/Prov.: _____ Zip/Postal Code: _____

*New York residents remit applicable sales taxes.
 Canadian residents remit applicable GST and provincial taxes.

HBACK-AJ